CELG

WHAT HAPPENS IN NASHVILLE

Claire Buchan is hardly over the moon about travelling to Nashville, Tennessee for her sister's hen party: a week of honky-tonks, karaoke and cowboys. Certainly not strait-laced Claire's idea of a good time, what with her lawyer job and sensible boyfriend, Philip. But then she doesn't bank on meeting Rafe Cavanna. On the surface, Rafe fits the cowboy stereotype, with his handsome looks and roguish charm. But as he and Claire get to know each other, she realises there is far more to him than meets the eye . . .

ANGELA BRITNELL

WHAT HAPPENS IN NASHVILLE

Complete and Unabridged

LINFORD
Leicester

First published in Great Britain in 2014 by
Choc Lit Limited
Surrey

First Linford Edition
published 2018
by arrangement with
Choc Lit Limited
Surrey

A catalogue record for this book is available
from the British Library.

ISBN 978–1–4448–3682–0

Published by
F. A. Thorpe (Publishing)
Anstey, Leicestershire

Set by Words & Graphics Ltd.
Anstey, Leicestershire
Printed and bound in Great Britain by
T. J. International Ltd., Padstow, Cornwall

This book is printed on acid-free paper

1

One glance at the hotel's faded blue paintwork and Claire's expectations took a nosedive. 'Down and Dirty in Nashville' — the name plainly applied to their accommodation as well as the dubious five-day package they'd foolishly signed up for. *Trust Heather.* Plainly her sister's brain had been softened by listening to far too much country music while dreaming of hot cowboys to flirt with before settling down to married life.

Claire grasped her suitcase handle and slung her carry-on bag back over her shoulder before heading towards the front door. She stepped inside the small lobby, grateful for the cooler air, and approached a square antique table topped with a laptop computer and phone. Presumably this served as the reception desk but there was no one in sight to greet her and no bell to ring for service. A nagging jet-lag headache pressed at her skull needing the immediate attention of a hot shower and a clean bed, neither of which she was convinced she'd find here. She tried to be fair — things might be shabby but there was no evidence of actual dirt.

She dropped her bags and set off in search of another human being. To the right of the elegant curved staircase she noticed a glass door and wandered over to peer out through into a small garden. On the wrought iron bench in the centre of the grass a man with a black cowboy hat tipped down over his face was stretched out with his long bare legs hanging out over one end, swigging beer straight from the bottle. *Wonderful. Very classy.*

Claire pushed the door open and stepped out onto the grass, the warm scent of honeysuckle immediately arousing her senses. She stopped still for a few seconds and admired the containers of colourful summer flowers dotted around the edges of the small lawn then took a few more steps. Nothing about the man's inert figure registered her arrival.

'Excuse me, do you work here?'

'Depends who's asking.' His deep laconic drawl trickled over her hot skin and Claire struggled to keep her focus.

'Are you drunk?'

He pushed the hat up some and because of his dark sunglasses she couldn't be sure, but Claire had the unsettling sensation of being thoroughly checked out.

'Nope, are you always this rude?'

'Would you mind removing your sunglasses while we speak?'

'Yep, I sure would. The sun's bright if you hadn't noticed, honey.'

Honey? 'Fine. I'll assume you work here as no one else appears to be around. Would it be too much trouble for you to come inside and check me in?' Claire's sarcasm only had a minimal effect as he slowly sat up, and

3

stopped to finish off his beer before standing up. The stranger's large, broad-shouldered frame took her by surprise and she instantly stepped backwards.

He chuckled, a rich warm laugh which seeped into her blood. 'Don't worry, sugar, I only eat innocent tourists on Tuesdays.' He held up his arm and made a point of checking the date on his watch. 'Damn, hadn't realised what day it was.'

'Have you quite finished?' Claire's scathing tone worked on most men but this one only flashed a wide grin, his far-too-perfect white teeth gleaming against his tanned skin.

'Sure am sorry, ma'am. The sun must've fried my brain.' He didn't sound the slightest bit apologetic but she nodded. He stood back to let her walk first and Claire strode off, certain his eyes were checking her out as he followed close behind.

* * *

4

Rafe remembered his brother's admonishment before he left his precious hotel in his tender care for a couple of weeks. *Guests are always right, even when they're wrong. Don't be your usual acerbic, rude self. And don't hit on any guests.* The last statement must have been Anton's attempt at a joke because they both knew that wasn't his style, especially these days. He guessed the order applied to sharp-tongued Brits as well as normal people.

He stepped behind the desk, removed his hat and slipped his sunglasses into the neck of his T-shirt before opening up the reservations screen. 'Name?'

'Claire Buchan. You should have a room for me from tonight, and I'll be joined by the other five members of the group on Thursday. We're booked in for your 'Down and Dirty in Nashville' package.'

Her lips pursed which was a definite shame as she had a lush mouth, the sort men wrote poems about, if they were the poetic kind, which he wasn't.

5

Despite her whiff of disapproval a fleeting wisp of sympathy tugged at Rafe. The package did sound tacky although Anton assured him they were doing booming business with the new craze for ever more unusual pre-wedding jaunts.

'Right.' Rafe checked the list and nodded. 'No problem. Do you have your credit card?'

As she opened her wallet and passed a card over their fingers brushed, sending a jolt of heat zinging through him. *Steer clear, you idiot.* Quickly he filled in the details and held the card back out, tossing her a challenging stare — wondering in a small corner of his brain whether she'd felt it too. Claire Buchan didn't flinch, pinning him to the ground with her clear light green eyes, piercing enough to cut glass. Without a word she snatched the card away.

Rafe pushed her key across the desk. 'The elevator's over there but I'm afraid it's broken, should be up and running later if the guy turns up to fix it.'

'Wonderful.'

Her dry sarcasm amused him. He appreciated sharp humour in a woman but it was often a fruitless search among their puzzling concerns about shoes and candle fragrances. 'Hey, you're young and fit.' Under the dowdy mud-coloured dress he was pretty sure there lurked a more than decent figure. 'A couple flights of stairs won't kill you, plus if you ask sweetly I'll even carry your bags up.'

'I can manage perfectly well, thank you.'

'It's part of my job, I'll take them,' he retorted and walked back out around. Rafe bent to pick up her matching dark green leather case and bag from the floor but she dove for them at the same time and tried to tug them away. He gave one strong yank and pulled them from her hands, hit by a wave of intoxicating spicy perfume rising from her fair skin. 'My God, are you always this stubborn?'

'Fetch the manager for me right now. I can't imagine why you're employed to deal with guests — or maybe you don't have any others, which wouldn't be a surprise,' she snapped, and Rafe burst out laughing.

He couldn't help himself, but the more he let rip the harder her features became until they resembled the granite countertops in the kitchen. 'Go ahead and complain, sugar, I'm listening.'

'What on earth do you mean?' She frowned. 'I thought there wouldn't be too much of a language barrier here but I was clearly wrong. Whoever taught you English should be shot.'

'That'd be my mother, and I'd give my last dollar to see you try — she's won more target competitions than you've had hot dinners, sweetheart.' A complete lie but riling this woman was fun, the most he'd had in ages.

'Why am I not surprised?'

Her haughty reply resonated with overtones of Queen Victoria and made

8

it hard for him to rein in his humour. 'Back to your original request, honey — the name's Rafe Cavanna and I am the manager. You comin' or not?' He stared her down, relishing the fact he'd shut her up for a minute. Rafe strode off up the stairs, not giving her much choice but to follow. At the top of the first flight he stopped to catch his breath.

'Too much for you?' Her fake sweetness brought him to the brink of swearing.

'What the devil have you got in here, bricks?'

She tossed her head back, exposing her long elegant neck and drawing his attention to the pale lightly freckled skin disappearing down into the demure neckline of her dress. He swallowed hard.

'Books.' A rush of heat flooded her cheeks, but she didn't apologise.

'A whole damn library?'

'Enough to keep me occupied.'

I could keep you occupied without resorting to books.

Claire Buchan's shocked expression made him aware he'd spoken out loud. *Shit.*

'Sorry,' he mumbled and turned away before he could screw up any worse.

* * *

Claire pushed the door shut behind him and leaned against it. How could any man be so appallingly rude and hot at the same time? The knot in her stomach tightened more, the one he'd put there the moment he peeled off his sunglasses and fixed her with the darkest blue eyes she'd ever seen. Eyes that could make a woman think and do things she shouldn't — especially one who was as good as engaged. She opened her handbag and found the small photo of Philip she'd brought with her — setting it in a prominent spot on the bedside table.

Philip, a respectable banker, wouldn't be seen dead wearing denim cut-off shorts, a sleeveless black T-shirt and cheap flip-flops. Of course he didn't have the tanned skin and muscles to show them off and unfortunately Mr Cavanna did — in spades, trowel loads of them if she was honest. One touch of his strong hand with its sprinkling of dark hair was all it'd taken to turn her insides to mush. It was a surprise — nothing like that had happened to her before. Heather would laugh her head off if Claire didn't get control of herself before Thursday.

Her younger sister always made fun of Philip, saying he was boring, mind-numbingly responsible and set in his ways. She couldn't dispute Heather's summing up but knew that many of her colleagues would describe her the same way. One evening Philip drew up a list of pros and cons on the subject of marriage but love didn't get a mention and when she commented on the omission he chided her and said they weren't star-crossed teenagers in a Shakespeare play. But every time Claire

11

saw Heather and her fiancé, Tom, together she felt so envious she could scream. She wanted what they had and wasn't sure she could settle for less any longer.

Although it was only six o'clock Nashville time she was beyond exhausted and stripped off her travel-stained clothes, abandoning the idea of unpacking properly until the morning. Five minutes later the hottest, most powerful shower of her life pounded her into submission. She dried off and wrapped the thin towel around her to wander back to the bedroom and find her nightdress. Then she was suddenly startled by a loud knock at the door.

'Who is it?'

'Rafe. You left your credit card at the desk.'

'Put it in the safe please and I'll collect it in the morning.'

'I'd rather pass it over to you now, I don't want any more misunderstandings.' His self-deprecating comment made her smile against her will and she crept closer to the door. Opening it back a few inches she stuck her hand out.

'Thank you.'

'Uh, if you don't mind opening up a touch more I brought you a tray of tea by way of apology.'

Claire followed his request without thinking until she met his bold stare, suddenly aware of her dress, or lack of it. A searing hot blush crept up from her toes to the top of her head and she clutched at the skimpy towel.

He pushed away a lock of floppy black hair, surprisingly streaked with grey, from his eyes. 'I was a jerk earlier. Don't know what came over me.' His husky voice rattled her and for a second she couldn't reply. 'I usually have manners. I hope we can start again?'

Start what? The question hung between them and her all-over blush intensified. 'Of course.' She snatched the tray, thanked him and slammed the door in his face for the second time.

2

Rafe struck out at the jangling alarm clock and winced as it crashed to the bare wood floor. After years of medical training and suffering the long hours of a junior doctor he should be used to having his sleep disturbed but he'd gotten soft. Regular hours at the children's clinic meant he rarely surfaced before six these days after a good eight hours' rest. Visions of Claire Buchan, wrapped in one of the hotel's pathetic towels with the heat and perfume rising from her skin tormented him all night. He'd been celibate long enough to know his painfully aroused body wouldn't kill him, but it was still a lousy way to start the day.

He dragged himself from the bed and hauled his sorry ass into the shower. Breakfast was available to guests from seven until ten and strained his culinary talents to the seams. Anton insisted everything be homemade and fresh to differentiate themselves from the other cut-price hotels in the area who relied on bitter coffee and pre-packaged mini-doughnuts.

Mentally he reckoned how many he'd have to deal with today. The one elderly couple staying only ate fruit and oatmeal and drank weak decaf coffee, the businessman from Atlanta wolfed down sausage and biscuits with gravy, and apart from that it was only his nemesis from the night before. No doubt she was the fussy sort. *Yeah, that's why she looked at you like something the cat dragged in.*

Rafe dried off and selected a pair of clean khakis and a pressed white shirt. He'd been caught out the day before in his oldest clothes, but there'd been no one around and his Italian side had craved the hot sun. He rejected the flip-flops and pulled on black socks and polished dress shoes.

He should've made time for a haircut

but tried his best to tame his hair, giving his reflection a rueful look. The thick, grey streaks that'd appeared almost overnight sliced memories into him every day, even after three long years. Time blurred the edges of the pain, but forgetting was never going to happen and deep down he didn't want it to.

Get a grip.

Rafe shoved his phone, keys and wallet in his pockets and stalked from the room. First move had to be getting the coffee made. He could drink any sludge going but for the guests he'd been ordered to fiddle around with grinding beans and all the palaver Anton insisted on.

He wandered outside and picked up the day's newspapers from the driveway. The front of the hotel was shabby and next on Anton's improvement list when there was some spare money. This afternoon he'd work on getting the windows washed then tomorrow he'd make a start on freshening up the paint

16

— it'd be small thanks to the brother who'd basically saved his life. The sound of footsteps made him turn and the breath sucked from his body.

Inches away from him stood Claire in skimpy red athletic shorts and a sleeveless top, glistening with sweat and breathing heavily. She bent down to stretch and his blood pressure soared to borderline stroke levels. He shamelessly ogled as she raised her arms above her head, the action making her generous breasts press against the damp fabric. Suddenly her eyes flew open.

'Good morning, Mr Cavanna. Enjoying the view?'

'Very much, Miss Buchan, and I guess you're enjoying the wonderful Tennessee humidity?' He followed the progress of one drop of sweat as it trickled down the front of her thin shirt. *Raphael, be a gentleman.* His father's voice remonstrated with him and he briefly felt ashamed.

'It's rather different from England.'

'Must be.' Rafe itched to ask about

17

her life there but it wasn't his business and he wasn't about to make it so either. He checked the time. 'I'd better get on with breakfast. Do you have any particular favourites? I can do pretty much anything with eggs, bacon, sausage, pancakes, biscuits . . . but I can whip up something healthier if you prefer?'

'I'm sure you can.' The teasing lilt to her voice took him by surprise. 'I'll take anything you fix. Breakfast is always my biggest meal of the day. About eight o'clock if it suits you.'

'Yeah, sure,' he grunted and made a quick escape before he could get himself in any more damn trouble.

* * *

Well, you did a good job there, girl, and frightened him off. She'd flirted. Claire didn't do flirting. Ever. Her rare relationships were with men she'd chosen with great care and she considered each step forward with

18

extreme caution. Heather's comment when she was trying to convince Claire Nashville would be an ideal spot for the party stuck in her mind.

No one we know goes there and it's a fun city with lots happening. We can have a good time and it won't go any further. Remember the adage — what happens in Vegas stays in Vegas? Well, we're going to apply it to Nashville. Anything we do there stays there. We'll never talk about it again. Think about it, Claire. For once in your life you won't have to be responsible.

Heather had never had to be the responsible one so what did she know? Five years younger, blonde and with a carefree bubbly personality, she'd been doted on by their father and protected by Claire all the time she was growing up. To give her credit she was a wonderful teacher but outside of the classroom she flitted through life seemingly unscathed and now had Tom adoring her too.

The idea of stepping outside of her

regimented box was tempting, but she couldn't see herself tossing away thirty-one years of watching out for other people and doing the right thing. Rafe Cavanna definitely didn't come under the heading of 'the right thing.' This morning, freshly shaved and smartly dressed, smelling of something masculine and woodsy when they got close, he'd still retained an air of danger not far under the smooth surface. What he was doing running a struggling hotel was a mystery. Something didn't fit and she was good at finding out things people didn't want to confess.

Back up in her room she showered and surveyed the contents of her meagre wardrobe. Glancing at Philip's photo she experienced a quick flash of guilt for caring about what to wear for breakfast so threw on a pair of simple navy linen trousers and a plain white T-shirt.

Downstairs she followed the wonderful aroma of cooking and found herself in a charming room freshly decorated in yellow and white, with about half a dozen tables only one of which was occupied by an older couple. The crisp white tablecloths and flowers everywhere gave a much better impression and made her hope this might not be a complete disaster after all.

Rafe swept in from the kitchen and her heart raced as his presence sucked all the air from the room. He set the couple of plates he was carrying down in front of the couple, chatting to them in a completely different way than he had to her last night — affable and totally devoid of sarcasm.

'Take a seat wherever you like, Miss Buchan,' he called over. 'Oh, and tea or coffee?' A definite sparkle lurked in his deep, dark eyes.

'I'll take a chance on your tea again.' He flashed a satisfied smile as if she'd agreed to taking a chance on far more than boiling water and a teabag. Quickly she looked away and sat down at the nearest table.

'There we go.' He appeared at her

side with a pretty china teapot and matching milk jug. 'Your breakfast will be ready in a couple of minutes.'

Claire took a few calming breaths as he disappeared. She disliked being unduly disturbed by any man and the way this one ricocheted between sarcasm, flirting and formal politeness unnerved her.

'Tennessee country ham, sausage, scrambled eggs, biscuits, fried apples, butter and homemade peach preserves.' He set down the massive plate and flashed another wolfish smile. 'Think that'll keep body and soul together?'

'Maybe. I'll let you know.'

'You do that, sweetheart.' With a long, slow wink he sauntered off and she sunk back into the chair, sorely tempted to run off upstairs unfed.

One bite of salty ham tossed that idiotic idea out the window, last night's missed dinner came back to haunt her as she shovelled food in a very unladylike fashion to satisfy her gnawing hunger.

'I brought you some more tea, but perhaps you'd prefer a Hoover?'

Claire jerked up to meet his blatant laughter and tried to appear stern and unamused but failed miserably. Philip never made fun of her. 'I don't hear you being abusive to your other guests, why me?' she challenged with a quick smile.

He froze and the pulse in his neck throbbed. Just as she thought he might reply he turned and walked away. What was that about?

* * *

Rafe rested his trembling hands on the kitchen counter. If he'd answered her Claire would've had every right to hit him or sue him for sexual harassment. This was madness. Apart from a couple of one-night stands out of the country at medical conferences he'd done without any semblance of a private life for three years. Until Claire walked out into the garden yesterday it hadn't been a problem but something about the

23

sight of her, so controlled and con-
tained, her subtle beauty teasing him
along with her sharp words, shook his
resolve and stirred feelings he'd long
ago laid to rest. At least he thought he
had. But Claire didn't behave like a
beautiful woman and when she'd flirted
earlier he could've sworn she was as
shocked as he was.

All he had to do was survive today
and then the rest of her group of
giggling women would arrive and he'd
be off the hook. In Anton's detailed
timetable his job was to taxi them
around some and make sure they were
in the right places at the right times.
Surely between plenty of cold showers
and avoidance he could manage not to
pounce on Claire? The problem was
this wasn't only about sex — he wanted
to discover what made her tick, talk to
her, share a laugh and not be so damn
lonely all the time.

*Stop feeling sorry for yourself,
moron. Everything that happened was
your own fault. Live with it.*

'Excuse me.'

Rafe jerked around, damping down a curse as he met Claire's worried frown. She hovered in the doorway, seeming uncertain whether to come on in.

'Are you all right?'

'Fine, why wouldn't I be?' he retorted.

'Uh, maybe because you're squeezing the glass in your hand so tight I'm afraid you're going to break it?'

He glanced down, staring at the offending object and wondered how and when it got there. Very carefully he set it on the counter and forced his fingers to relax so it stayed there when he let go. Rafe shoved his hands in his pockets. 'Did you want something?' He hated sounding so rude but couldn't stand a foot away from her smelling her light floral perfume, overlaid with hints of his mother's summer camellias, without longing to kiss her wide, unadorned mouth.

'I wondered when it might be convenient to discuss the agenda for our time here. I want everything lined up before tomorrow.'

Rafe cleared his throat and tried to get his brain back into gear. 'I've got the plans. How about after I've cleared up from breakfast? About ten-ish?'

'That'll work. Where do you want me?'

'We could have coffee out in the garden.' Fresh air might help his case, he was desperate enough to try anything.

'That'll work.' She turned to leave with a swish of her neat ponytail and glanced back over her shoulder with a mischievous smile. 'By the way, thanks for breakfast, it was delicious and will definitely do me for a couple of hours.'

'Glad to hear it.' He made himself shut up and not make another sassy remark about her eating habits. In truth it was a relief to come across a woman who enjoyed her food instead of picking at a lettuce leaf. 'That's the extent of my culinary talents which is why we don't serve lunch or dinner,' he explained.

'You're far more talented than I am. I'm close friends with all the microwave dinners available and I've got my favorite takeaway places on speed dial.' Her careless laugh rippled through him, her self-confidence in admitting her failings attracting him as much as her body had earlier. 'I'd better leave you to work. See you later.'

Rafe managed a nod as she left the kitchen, struck dumb again. If he'd wanted to impress her he was doing a lousy job. But he didn't so no problem. *Right. Not much you don't.*

3

Claire watched Rafe from the lobby, enjoying the fact he wasn't yet aware of her presence. She'd considered changing into something cooler for sitting outside but was afraid it might create the wrong impression — or the right one — either way was bad.

Today he sat on the bench reading a newspaper with no expanse of tanned skin and muscles visible, but the more conservative clothes did nothing to alleviate the pull he'd worked on her since the second they met. She tended to analyse everything but he defied all attempts to find a logical explanation for her weakness. Before she could push the door open he glanced over and beckoned.

Claire sucked in a deep breath and stepped into the dappled sunlight, feeling rather like a fly tempted into a spider's web. A slow smile crept across his stern face as he gestured for her to sit by him. Without any other chairs around she had no choice.

'Black or white?'

'Black or white what?'

He smirked and pointed to the coffee pot balanced on the wicker table. 'What did you think?'

'I don't know.' She was cross at being caught not paying attention. 'We always seem to talk at cross purposes.'

'So which is it to be?' He raised the pot and his eyes weren't hidden behind sunglasses today so she couldn't avoid their dangerous challenge.

'Black, please.' Perhaps a good dose of caffeine would sort out her tired brain. Claire took the cup he poured and sipped the steaming liquid. 'You make decent coffee too, I'm impressed. All I do is pour boiling water on a spoonful of instant granules.'

'That's my usual go to as well, but . . . I make it properly for guests.' His slight hesitation made her wonder what he'd really been going to say.

'Your garden is lovely.' She glanced around, searching for an innocuous topic to discuss until they got down to business.

'I can't take the credit. This is my brother's doing and his wife.'

'Do they help around the hotel?'

'It belongs to Anton and Poppy but I'm managing it while they're on vacation.' He glanced away and shifted in the seat. Claire couldn't imagine why explaining that made him so awkward.

'I'm sure they're grateful.'

'They may not be if I make a mess of things.' He cracked a reluctant smile.

'What's your normal job?'

Rafe fiddled with his coffee mug. 'Oh, this and that.' His obvious lie made her cross. 'How about you?' he smoothly changed the subject.

'I'm a barrister, I prosecute criminal cases at the Crown Court in Exeter, that's in the south of England.' His dark eyebrows rose but he didn't speak. 'And yes, I know I can be intimidating and don't tolerate liars gladly.'

Rafe pushed away the rogue lock of hair he was forced to do continual battle with and fixed his gaze on her. 'Is that a warning?'

'Take it how you like.' She tossed out the challenge and waited. All he did was give her a long slow nod and return to sipping his coffee. 'Right,' she snapped, 'how about we get on with this so we don't waste any more of either of our days?'

He set the cup down and picked up a manila folder from the table. Rafe reached into his shirt pocket to bring out a pair of square black-rimmed glasses and slipped them on with a wry smile. 'No point in pretending I can read without them.' Did he have to be so disarmingly sexy? 'Down and Dirty in Nashville,' he opened the folder and read.

'Why'd you give it that dreadful name?' she interrupted and a small grin tugged at his tempting mouth.

'Blame Anton and Poppy. They came

up with the bright idea and apparently it sells well. Got you here didn't it?'

Claire bristled. 'Not really. This is my sister's choice. It certainly wouldn't be mine. She's a huge country music fan for reasons beyond my comprehension, and is getting married in three weeks. I was nominated to organise the trip which is why I came early.'

'You didn't want any screw-ups on your watch, right?'

His casual comment struck her deep in the gut. Despite her father's assurance she'd always blamed herself for her mother leaving them and overcompensated ever since by being a perfectionist in everything she did. Claire managed to nod and he didn't make any inane reply. Rafe began to run through the timetable for each day and when he stopped five minutes later she realised she hadn't paid attention to anything but his smooth, deep drawl. It reminded her of the warm golden syrup her mother used to pour over their Shrove Tuesday pancakes, and she felt sure she could happily listen to him speak for hours even if it was only reading from the phone book.

'So it all sounds okay to you, sugar?'

She'd caught a few actual words — mentions of honky-tonks, a barbecue, karaoke and the Opry. Baffling to her, but she guessed it'd keep Heather happy which was all that mattered.

'How are we getting to all these places?' She struggled to ask a sensible question but he broke into a broad grin so she guessed he'd told her already. Very patiently he explained the hotel had an eight-seater van and he'd drive them, dropping them off and picking them up when they were done.

'Except for Opry night when you get limo service.'

Claire struggled to come across as her usual efficient self. 'That all seems in order. You're collecting them from the airport tomorrow, right?'

'Yep,' he nodded, 'there's room if you want to come along.'

Did she want to commit to being on

her own with him? *Don't be an idiot. He's talking about a short drive in rush-hour traffic, not slow dancing in a dark nightclub.* Claire's blood ran hot at the idea of his arms wrapped around her, pulling her close . . .

'Yes, or no?'

A rush of heat flooded her face. 'Yes, please.'

'Good.' He closed the folder and put his pen away. As he removed the glasses she gave a little sigh. 'Is something wrong?'

'They suit you.' The words tumbled out before she could hold back. *Act a little more juvenile, why don't you?* Claire jumped up and shoved her hand out at him. 'Thank you for your help. I'm sure it'll all go smoothly.' He grasped her hand, not shaking it but wrapping his long fingers around and holding on. A surge of heat raced through her body, pooling in places she shouldn't even be aware existed around this dangerous man.

Claire pulled away and stumbled on

the grass, righting herself before he could help. Without another word she stalked off back inside, not needing to turn around to know he was watching her — again.

★ ★ ★

They suit you? Rafe wasn't sure how he felt knowing she might be equally interested in him. While he believed she disliked him it was easier to keep his desire for her in check but those three words turned things upside down. Her earlier touch of flirtation hadn't struck him as serious, but the way she'd looked at him a few minutes ago with her light green eyes shimmering shook him to the core. And when she'd offered her hand Rafe knew he'd clutched it too damn hard, wrapping her soft warm skin with his rougher fingers and craving much more.

Physical work usually did the trick and took his mind off things it didn't need to be brooding over so Rafe

35

picked up the tray and set off inside. A spate of window washing should do the trick.

★ ★ ★

Six hours later he admitted defeat. After finishing the windows he'd scraped paint and sanded, ready to repaint tomorrow, but still wasn't exhausted. He'd even gone out to buy groceries, remembering soy milk for the fussy new guest — a Californian here for a couple of nights — and re-laid the breakfast tables. But now here he was back in the garden, freshly showered and with a beer in hand, and still — as his southern to the bone maternal grand-mother would've said — nervous as a long-tailed cat in a room full of rocking chairs.

'Excuse me for disturbing you but can you point me in the direction of the nearest restaurant?'

Claire appeared in front of him and Rafe stared, he knew he did, but couldn't stop. She'd released her light brown hair from its tight ponytail to curl softly around her shoulders. Her slim-fitting dress wasn't the prettiest of colours — a light grey instead of a warmer shade of pink or gold to flatter her pale skin, but it was short enough to show off the long legs he'd admired this morning. She'd even added a touch of something pink and glossy to her generous mouth. For both their sakes he wished she hadn't.

'Mr Cavanna, did you hear me?'

Her sharp tone broke through his daydreams. 'Sorry, I was miles away. A restaurant, did you say?'

'Yes,' she sighed, her patience obviously wearing thin. 'It's seven o'clock and I'm hungry, it seemed a logical place to consider going.'

He relaxed into a smile and she grinned right back, lightening up her serious face and showing off a dimple he hadn't noticed before, tucked into the right side of her pretty mouth. 'Yeah, I guess it would be.' He ran his gaze over her, thought for a second about his brother's joking warning, but spoke up anyway. 'I haven't eaten yet. Don't suppose you'd care to join me?'

'You said you don't cook dinner?'

'Did you hear me offering to?' He tossed right back and she rewarded him with another smile. 'No, you didn't. I was considering getting Chinese if that suits you.' *I was planning to drink a few more beers and eat peanut butter and crackers later, but I'll tell another small lie if it gets me a couple of hours with you.* 'I can pick some up from around the corner and there's wine in the fridge.'

She nibbled at her lip and he guessed she was fighting with the same qualms.

'It's just dinner. We both need to eat, sweetheart.'

'All right, as long as you're sure I'm not interrupting your plans?'

'Does watching reruns of *Andy Griffith* count?'

'Who's he?'

Rafe chuckled. 'Heathen. It's an old

38

TV series. Andy's the epitome of the old rural South, a small-town sheriff with traditional values and a cute son called Opie. I can see I've got a lot to teach you, honey.'

'I'm only here for five days,' she said steadily.

'Better make the most of them then, hadn't we?' he said, while knowing he shouldn't, and she blushed.

4

'Help yourself, and don't be shy,' Rafe teased and she playfully stuck out her tongue. Claire grabbed the carton from him and dumped a couple of heaped spoonfuls of sweet and sour chicken on top of her fried rice. 'I like a woman with a healthy appetite.' His deep drawl sent shivers through Claire's body and it was all she could do not to grab him across the table, but her sensible side reasserted itself.

'Stop it.'

'What?' Rafe leaned forward, rested his elbows on the table and stared into her with such intensity she swallowed hard to steady her breathing.

'You know exactly what I mean — the double entendres and looking at me as though I'm a ripe piece of fruit ready to fall from the tree.'

Suddenly he covered her right hand

with his, rubbing his long fingers in tempting circles over her trembling skin. 'At least I'm not the one sending out mixed signals.'

Claire frowned. 'Is that what I've been doing?'

'Sure have, honey.' His finger trailed up and down her arm and it was a struggle to hold on to her common sense. All she kept thinking was how wonderful it'd be to have his big competent hands roam all over her.

Guilt slammed into her. She'd crossed the line between light flirtation and so much more. 'Look, I'm sorry, it's my fault. I've got a serious boyfriend at home and I didn't mean to . . . ' Her voice trailed away as Rafe's features turned to stone. He withdrew his hand as if she'd scalded him.

'I've a real short list of moral rules, but one is never messing with another man's woman.'

'I'm my own woman, no one else's, and never will be. What rock did you crawl out from under?' Claire pushed her plate away and jumped up, shoving the chair so hard it fell with a crash to the floor.

'I've plenty of faults, honey, but being dishonourable isn't one of them.'

She froze as he stood too and closed the gap between them, the waves of heat pulsing from his body luring her forward. 'You misunderstand me,' Claire whispered, laying her hands against his broad chest to stop him, or her, from taking another step. 'I'm disappointed in myself, I shouldn't . . . want this.'

'You wanna tell me about him?'

She shook her head, but proceeded to do exactly what he'd asked. The blank expression on his face never changed as she told about meeting Philip five years ago. 'We're very much alike. We think everything through and never act on impulse. Before I came here he asked me to consider living with him. If it goes well we'll contemplate marriage.'

'Exciting.' His scathing tone irritated her.

'I prefer to know where I stand, plus I haven't decided yet if it'd be a wise move.'

Rafe's searing gaze drifted down to linger on her mouth and unconsciously she licked her lips. 'Not sure I'd want to be considered any woman's 'wise move.''

Without thinking Claire burst out laughing. 'I don't think you need to be concerned about that, it's very unlikely.' This man with his brooding good looks, sharp tongue, and air of mystery wouldn't be any woman's sensible choice.

'You'd better go. I'll clear up.' His taut, clipped words told her she'd pushed far enough.

'I really am sorry. I've behaved badly.' Claire couldn't bear to look at him any more and turned away. Rafe grasped her arm from behind and she jerked to a halt.

'Would one kiss be a fatal mistake?' His husky voice up against the back of her neck made the hairs tingle and sent a rush of heat racing through her body. Rafe's searching fingers slid under her hair, lifting it out of the way before his hot mouth pressed into her exposed skin. His tongue slid expert teasing licks and Claire's knees buckled under the slow assault to her senses. As his other hand moved to cradle her waist he pulled her back against his steel-hard body holding her up. 'It's not enough. Knew it wouldn't be.'

'It's got to be,' she gasped, and instantly he loosened his grip.

'Hell, I'm sorry. I don't know what got into me. It's my turn to apologise.' The sorrow in his voice tore at her and she quickly took a couple of steps to reach the door. Only then did she let herself glance back. Rafe's full-on stare was so full of naked longing a cry lodged in her throat. No man had ever looked at her that way before.

Claire forced herself to run.

*   *   *

The knowledge she could've been his for the taking didn't improve Rafe's

44

mood. Claire had told him she had a steady boyfriend so he shouldn't have flirted in the first place let alone kiss her. He could never put another man through what he'd suffered in the past. Of course Claire hadn't known what she'd come so close to asking him to do and it was bullshit to tell himself it was simply the result of being without a woman too long.

The deep craving she'd stirred in him upset the balance he'd fought so long to achieve. He considered indulging in an excess of whisky or the sleeping pills he always kept in reserve, but rejected both in an instant which was a distinct improvement on the bad old days.

Rafe forced himself back to the table and went through the mechanics of clearing away the remains of their disastrous dinner. He tossed the white boxes in the trash and washed their plates and cutlery. Picking up her wine glass he ran his thumb over the pink lipstick smudge and his body tightened, it didn't take much to imagine how sweet and needy her mouth would've tasted.

Anger swept through him and Rafe raised his arm and hurled the glass, sending it shattering into the wall. A streak of red wine trickled down the white paint and a growl escaped the back of his throat. Damn Anton. He could hardly call his brother and tell him to cut his much needed vacation short because Rafe couldn't hack managing a few hotel guests and his newly stirred up libido.

He closed his eyes and took slow, deep breaths from the base of his stomach, filling his lungs before slowly exhaling. The angry mist cleared from his brain and his muscles loosened.

Sleep wouldn't come tonight, but he was used to that by now and it hadn't killed him yet.

*   *   *

Claire laid back against the soft white pillows and smiled at Heather's latest

46

text from her hotel near Heathrow airport. In theory the girls were getting a good night's sleep before flying tomorrow but they'd already started partying. By the increasingly incoherent nature of the messages Claire guessed an excess of wine was involved.

Checked out the local talent for us yet?

You're getting married remember. Claire's pointed reply was half aimed at herself.

Only talking about looking and having fun. Anyway you didn't answer me.

Rafe, kissing her neck, his dark blue eyes sliding over her, and his uber-sexy drawl — if she hinted at anything her sister would go wild. Heather would flat out encourage her because she thought Philip the dreariest man on the planet and couldn't believe Claire was even considering marrying him. They'd had a heated discussion on the subject before she left when Heather asked outright if Claire loved Philip. She'd been unable to lie outright and ended the argument by walking away.

I'm resting at the hotel to get over jet lag. She tapped in an evasive reply, not adding that it was in between dangerous confrontations with their host.

Boring. Wait until we get there. We'll shake things up.

I'm sure you will. *Get some sleep. See you tomorrow.*

You too. Spoilsport.

Claire turned her phone off with a sigh and laid it on the bedside table. She picked up Philip's picture and studied his open, frank smile. At first she'd gravitated towards him because of the very things now weighing her down. His utter steadiness in everything he did and said appealed to her but now their relationship had morphed into a boring routine that was driving her crazy. They did their washing together on Mondays to save on the water bill and always got takeaway pizza on Wednesdays when there was a two for one special. When she'd suggested changing things up one night and having Indian instead he'd looked at her as though she'd grown an extra head. He didn't care for public displays of affection and was gentle with her in private, taking it slow and easy. Philip's lovemaking didn't set her on fire but she was okay with that. *You were until Rafe touched you, sure you are now?*

One day in Rafe Cavanna's company and she was doubting everything, including her own common sense and self-control. If she hadn't said no tonight how far would they have gone?

She opened the drawer and slipped the silver-framed photo inside before softly closing it shut, not asking herself why. Claire pulled the sheet up to her chin and closed her eyes, determined to sleep instead of spending the whole night thinking about tomorrow and Rafe Cavanna.

★ ★ ★

Unwilling to use Anton and Poppy's bedroom amid all the signs of the

49

happy couple Rafe had appropriated one of the smaller guest rooms. Its almost monastic bareness appealed to him and he'd done almost nothing to brighten it for his short stay.

One thing he'd added to the top of the pine dresser was the last photo he had of the three of them — the family he'd lost because of his obsession with his old job. He made himself take it everywhere as a reminder although it wasn't necessary because they never really left his mind. Tonight it helped him to understand why he'd turned so vehemently on Claire. She knew nothing of him or his past and he intended on keeping it that way.

Tomorrow he'd be cool and polite and certainly wouldn't go within touching reach of the dangerous, tempting Brit. Pink pigs had better learn to fly real soon was all he knew.

5

Claire checked her appearance in the mirror and frowned. She'd never had much of an interest in fashion and being forced to wear conservative clothes for work, combined with a robe and wig for her court days, had provided her an easy way out for too long. The severe white-collared blouse and black tailored trousers she'd chosen today were a non-verbal statement to Rafe she meant what she'd said last night. She'd managed to avoid him all day but it was nearly time to leave for the airport and she couldn't put it off any longer.

Wandering out to the top of the stairs she glanced down into the lobby, her heart racing at the sight of him sprawled in one of the chairs reading, giving the impression of a big cat waiting for its prey. Slowly he lowered the newspaper and met her awkward half-smile before sweeping her from head to toe with his sharp eyes.

'Ready when you are, Miss Buchan. The van's outside.' Rafe stood and strode off out the front door before she could reply.

Claire didn't rush down the stairs from a childish desire to make him wait but slowly made her way to join him.

'Seat belt on,' he snapped as she got in and he immediately started up the engine. His brusque order riled her but she obeyed, determined to pay him back for his rudeness when she got the chance.

The cool blasts of air conditioning couldn't hide the scent of his distinctive cologne or the warmth emanating from his body mere inches away from hers so Claire wriggled closer to the door and fixed her eyes on the road.

'When we get there I'll drop you off outside, you can meet them by security and head down to the baggage area. I'll park and come join you.'

He drove the same way he did everything else, a little too fast and very sure. Claire sneaked a glance over at him as he navigated through the heavy traffic with ease and the tense set of his broad shoulders was the only clue to the fact he wasn't as immune to her company as he might appear. The knowledge made her smile to herself even though it shouldn't have.

'Thank you,' she said demurely.

'No problem.'

'I ought to give you a fair warning, they'll have a ton of luggage. My sister and her friends don't believe in travelling light.'

'Par for the course. Present company excepted, of course, apart from where books are concerned.'

His quick smile caught her unawares and the burst of simple good humour was such a surprise it hit her straight in the gut and she couldn't resist smiling right back. 'Of course.' Her voice trembled as she held his mesmerising gaze, still amazed blue eyes could be so dark. The heart-stopping moment only lasted a matter of seconds before he jerked his attention back to the road.

Claire slumped back into the seat for the rest of the drive, the sooner Heather and the rest of the gang arrived the better.

★　★　★

'O-M-G. Why didn't you tell me about the resident hunk?' Heather hissed. Claire followed her gaze towards the luggage carousel and saw Rafe handling all the bags as if they weighed nothing at all.

'What's to tell?'

'Uh, maybe the fact he's drop dead gorgeous. Don't pretend, Sis. You wanted to keep him for yourself.'

Claire's cheeks burned and she stumbled over how to reply without dropping herself in even deeper.

'Hit the nail on the head, didn't I? Has he made moves on you already, you lucky creature?' Heather poked her arm and gave another wicked grin.

'Of course not.' The lie tumbled out before she realised. One kiss on the back of the neck hardly counted — did it?

'Fine, if he hasn't he's fair game. Of course the others are drooling over your hot hotelkeeper too so there's going to be quite a queue.' Heather's raucous laugh rang out and Rafe stared at them both, his expression hard and unrevealing.

Another shot of heat lit up Claire's face. He'd obviously guessed they were talking about him. The hint of a smug smile tugged at the corners of his mouth and she wanted to smack him for being so vain. 'Feel free.' Claire tossed off a casual reply. 'Come on, traffic's bad this time of day.'

'What's on the agenda tonight?'

'Nothing. We thought you'd be tired after the journey.'

Heather's expression was scathing. 'I hope you're joking. I don't intend wasting one of our precious evenings in order to sleep. We'll discuss it in the van. I'm sure the gorgeous Mr Cavanna will have some ideas.'

No doubt.

'Come on girls, time to get the party started.' Heather waved her arms in the air and gave a loud yell. Everyone in the baggage area turned to stare at them and Claire's heart sank. This could be the longest five days of her life.

★   ★   ★

Rafe handed out keys and hauled bags up the stairs — all the while cursing the elevator repair man for still not turning up. Southern women could talk but these five were in a league of their own, except for Claire who'd pretty much let the others chatter on.

During the drive home they talked him into dropping them off on Broadway as soon as they changed clothes — he heard the words honky-tonk crawl and hot cowboys mentioned, spotting Claire's distaste in his rear-view mirror.

If he wasn't trying to ignore her, Rafe might almost feel sorry for the woman who'd torn him up and spat him out last night. Only almost.

'Give us an hour, Mr Cavanna and we'll be raring to go,' Heather Buchan instructed him with a broad smile before running off with her girlfriends. The idea she was Claire's sister was baffling, but he and Anton were chalk and cheese too — his older brother friendly and easy-going compared to his own prickly, acerbic personality.

He escaped to the kitchen to fortify himself with a sandwich and an extra-large mug of pitch-black coffee before his next chauffeuring duties. Rafe's phone buzzed and he checked to find a new message from Anton.

New group arrived okay? Be friendly and I don't care you think this is dumb. It's paying the bill for my vacation.

He responded in a positive, upbeat tone and tried not to gag.

* * *

57

Rafe controlled the urge to smile, mainly because it wasn't funny. Poor Claire stood out like a raven in a group of colorful parrots. The rest of the women wore skin-tight jeans or short skirts, sparkly tops leaving little to the imagination, and ankle-breaking heels, but not Claire. She wore the same black trousers and white shirt she'd had on earlier, flat shoes, and no make-up. Her beauty shouted out to him — her unadorned skin, soft gleaming hair, and unpainted lush lips — taking all his pitiful store of self-control to stop from yanking her away and saying she didn't have to do this. He made himself remember Philip.

'Okay, ladies. In you get.'

They tumbled into the van squabbling all the while over who'd sit where, and he resented his surge of disappointment when Claire ended up in the very back. Heather snagged the front passenger seat with a triumphant smile. He'd heard them all giggling and pointing at him earlier and guessed he was in for a whole boat load of trouble until he shunted them on the plane back to England.

'So, Mr Cavanna — or can I call you Rafe?' He had to nod or appear churlish, but kept his eyes on the traffic. 'I want to know all about you. Claire said your brother runs the hotel usually so what do you do? Have you always lived in Nashville? What do you enjoy doing in your spare time?'

'I promise I'm not very interesting. Grew up here and work around the place.' Meeting her curious stare he closed the conversation with a polite smile. 'Do y'all want me to pick you up later?'

Heather's long red nails rested on his bare arm and he itched to brush them away. 'I'll find out you know. My sister might be the lawyer of the family, but I'm far better at this sort of thing,' she teased.

You can try all you like, lady, you're wasting your time with me. If I can resist your gorgeous sister, you don't stand a hope in hell.

'We're nearly there. I'll find some-where to pull over and let y'all out,' he carried on, ignoring her completely. Rafe negotiated his way through the heavy traffic and crowds of tourists enjoying a lively downtown Thursday evening. He preferred the quieter venues where it was possible to listen to good music without having to put up with having beer dumped on him or being accosted by drunk women.

Heather flung open the door and jumped out onto the sidewalk. 'Come on girls.' They all tumbled out laughing except Claire who climbed slowly out as though she was going to her execution.

'Try to enjoy yourself, it's not that bad,' he attempted to reassure her and she threw him a grateful smile, putting an instant dent in his good intentions to keep a firm line between them.

'I will, don't worry. I won't spoil things for Heather.'

'I know. Hey, tell them to watch their

purses and . . . ' Rafe ached to tell her to stay away from glib, smooth-talking men, but it wasn't his place. 'What time do you want me to come back?'

Claire checked her watch. 'I don't know. I hate asking you to come out again. We could get a couple of taxis.'

'No,' he snapped and she looked puzzled. He'd rather suffer tomorrow from a lack of sleep than worry about her all evening.

'Okay,' she dragged out the word and slipped her bag, messenger style, across her chest. 'Is midnight too late?'

Rafe shook his head. 'Not a problem. If you need me earlier, or later, just call.' He fixed her with a hard stare, wanting her to know he meant every word.

She nibbled at her lip, and he ached to kiss her until they both forgot their own names. *She's got a boyfriend and you screw up relationships, end of story*. He turned away before he could say or do something stupid.

'Thanks. Really.' For a few seconds

she held his breath in her hands, then turned away, leaving him as crazy for her as ever.

6

After the third crowded bar they ended up at the famous Wildhorse Saloon and Claire resigned herself to the fact she'd never share her sister's love of all things country. Pippa, Emily, Cat and Helen were in full swing and making the most of the effect their English accents had on the locals. At each venue they'd been swarmed around by admirers and offered more free drinks than even they could manage. Claire's head pounded and she craved quiet and fresh air.

'Come on, the line dancing's starting and, as the bride-to-be, I'm ordering you to join in.' Heather shouted by her ear.

'I don't dance,' Claire insisted but her sister dragged her towards the small dance floor.

'You're an expert at following rules and they call all the moves out. Don't be a spoilsport,' Heather pleaded and she remembered Rafe's gentle urging to try to enjoy herself. Impulsively she hugged her sister, seeing a flare of surprise in her eyes.

'I won't spoil anything, promise.'

Heather gave her a curious look. 'I know. I appreciate this isn't your cup of tea.'

'No, but it is yours which is what's important so let's have fun,' Claire declared and slipped her arm through Heather's.

For the next hour she flung herself around with complete abandonment, being swung around by sweaty strangers and finding the fact she tripped over her own feet incredibly funny. Drinks kept appearing in her hand and if she hadn't been sticking to tonic water Claire would've thought herself drunk. She found Heather and draped an arm around her neck. 'What's next?'

'Next? It's nearly time to turn back into Cinders and be rescued by our very own Prince Charming.'

Claire pouted. 'Now who's the spoilsport?'

'You didn't try any of the cocktails, did you?' There'd been a long list of wildly alcoholic drinks with suggestive names on offer at each place they'd been and the other girls tried most of them. Heather leaned closer and sniffed. 'My God, you did, your breath smells like neat alcohol.'

'That's ridic . . . ridiculu . . . silly,' Claire stammered and burst into more giggles.

'Did Will give you any drinks?' She gestured towards the bar and Claire struggled to focus on the man she pointed out, a handsome blond with matching black cowboy boots and hat, who gave them a broad smile.

'Yes, he'd been dancing with you, so I thought . . . ' Her voice trailed away and a wave of tiredness swept over her.

'He's cute, but I worked out he's a bit naughty where drinks are concerned. I'm guessing he asked them to add a shot of vodka. I picked it up right away when he tried the same trick on me, but I'm not surprised he caught you out. We'd better get you home.'

'But I don't want to spoil . . . '

'You won't be.' Heather's firm voice startled Claire. 'It's been a long day and we've got several more to go. Anyway Pippa and the others are getting a little worse for wear. We need to pace ourselves.'

Later Claire would have to think about this new take-charge side of her sister but right now all she craved was her bed and a long uninterrupted sleep.

'I'll round them up and we'll head outside to find our chauffeur.' Heather shoved her arm firmly around Claire's wrist and hauled her around the room, shepherding all the others towards the door.

As she took a step outside the cooler night air hit her like a bucket of water in the face and her knees buckled. Strong arms appeared from somewhere and held her up.

'What the hell have you been doing?'

Rafe's cross voice penetrated the fog in her brain and she burst out laughing. 'I've been having fun, just like you told me to.'

'I didn't tell you to get drunk as a skunk,' he shouted back, his angry glare only making her laugh more.

'I ordered tonic water but Heather reckons her new friend added some vodka. It's not my fault.' She wrapped her arms around his neck. *Goodness. It was a long way up there*. The man always smelled so good; fresh, clean, and scrumptious enough to eat. Claire nuzzled into his skin and from some faraway place she heard him moan.

'The van's over here.' Before she could protest he swept her up into his arms and even in her confusion Claire felt safe and wriggled further into his embrace. The fresh air was having a beneficial effect now and her awareness trickled back. 'I'll put her up here with me, that way I can keep an eye on her if we need to stop.'

Plainly he thought she might throw up all over his precious vehicle. 'I only had a couple of drinks,' she protested.

'Do you normally drink to excess?' His sarcasm trickled through and she sagged into the seat.

'No. Did I tonight?'

Rafe's luscious mouth turned up in the hint of a smile. If she didn't kiss him soon she'd scream. Claire knew he'd be an excellent kisser. There'd be nothing sweet and gentle about Mr Cavanna's lovemaking.

'I'd guess you did, sweetheart. I'll dose you up with my fail-proof remedy of strong coffee, water and aspirin when we get to the hotel so you'll be okay in the morning.' The change in his voice startled her, the annoyed layer was gone replaced by something close to caring.

Claire rested her head on his shoulder and smiled. All was right with the world.

* * *

Alone with her in the kitchen Rafe knew he should've deposited Claire into her sister's care, rationalising his action — or inaction — by the fact Heather was busy shepherding the other four women to bed. Naturally it didn't have anything to do with the fact there was a softness about her he'd never seen before, with the prickly edges blurred to reveal what he suspected was the real Claire.

'Feeling better?' He rested his hand on her arm and she gazed at him far too thoughtfully for a half-drunk woman, her green eyes luminous in the faint light from over the sink.

'Much. I should go to bed.'

'Yeah.' Rafe stroked her soft skin without thinking what he was doing, craving the contact as badly as a thirsty man yearns for water. 'You want me to help you up the stairs?'

Claire's drowsy smile tugged something deep inside. 'I may be drunk, but even I know that'd be a terrible idea.'

Define terrible.

'You're a good man, Rafe.'

Her quiet words struck him to the core. She didn't have a clue. 'You don't know me,' he croaked, his hoarse voice barely emerging from his tight throat.

'I want to. More than anything.'

The ache deepened, and he considered telling her everything to see if she still thought he was a good man.

'I'd better say goodnight.' She rose to her feet and he automatically followed suit. Claire fixed her intense gaze on him, never moving, waiting. A faint hint of her perfume drifted his way and his resolve dropped away.

Rafe dared to rest the fingers of one trembling hand against her cheek, feeling the heat rise in her skin as he explored the curves of her face. 'You're so lovely.'

'Sure you're not the one who's drunk?' she teased.

'Drunk on you, sweetheart, drunk on you.'

She sighed and licked her lip. 'Kiss me, Rafe.'

'What about . . . ' Before he could mention Philip's name her mouth pressed against his, the first taste of her sweetness losing him. She teased him with the tip of her tongue and Rafe shoved his hands up through her soft, silky hair, clutching tight handfuls to hold her in place for what he intended to do. What he'd wanted from the instant she appeared in the garden; cool, haughty, and so tempting he'd fought against grabbing her on the spot.

He traced the outline of her lips, loving her small sounds of pleasure and the way her body unconsciously molded to his. Claire opened to his searching tongue, arching her throat as he explored her mouth. A sweeping roll of desire pounded his senses and he couldn't hold back any longer.

'Don't stop,' she gasped against his assault, flashing him a full-on sexy smile as he worked on the top button of her blouse, forcing it open before he started on the next.

'Right, let's see to my . . . ' Heather's

voice penetrated his brain and Rafe wrapped Claire in his arms in a gesture of protection. 'What the hell do you think you're doing taking advantage of her?'

Claire glanced over her shoulder. 'Calm down. Rafe wasn't doing anything I didn't ask for, and want.'

A scarlet rush of heat flamed Heather's face. 'You're drunk. You don't know what you . . . '

'Oh, yes, I do, and I'm not that out of it. Rafe took good care of me.'

Heather scoffed. 'Real good care by the look of it. What happened to my virtuous sister who kept telling me off for wanting to flirt a little?'

'It was only a kiss.'

Rafe swallowed hard but kept his mouth shut. They both knew she was lying.

'It wouldn't have been if I hadn't come in,' Heather yelled, her angry eyes flashing. 'Look at the state of you. He'd have had you naked over that table in another five minutes.'

72

Three. It wouldn't have taken five. He wasn't that slow.

'It's late. How about we all pack up for the night?' Rafe suggested and Heather glared at him. Obviously he was now on a par with a spraying skunk in her book.

'Good idea,' Claire murmured. 'Why don't you go on, Heather, and I'll be up in a few minutes?'

'Are you sure?'

He'd had enough of being treated like a potential rapist. 'Miss Buchan. I've never forced myself on any woman and don't plan to start tonight.'

Heather shook her head at him. 'I'm disappointed. I'd formed a higher opinion of you.'

'I hope you'll give me a chance to redeem myself.' The scathing note of sarcasm didn't appear to register as she gave him a tentative smile.

'We'll see. Good night, Mr Cavanna.' Heather fixed her attention back on Claire. 'Don't be long.' She strode away without another word, her high heels

73

clicking on the tiles.

Rafe stifled a laugh as Claire stuck out her tongue at her sister's retreating back. 'Now, now, behave yourself,' he whispered, as she threw her arms back around his neck.

'That was weird.'

'In what way, apart from getting caught I mean? You'd think we were teenagers.'

Claire played with his hair, sending shivers through him which had nothing to do with the fact the air conditioning had just kicked in. 'Responsible, critical sister is my role not Heather's. I'm mystified where this new side of her came from.'

'Maybe the same place as your . . . more relaxed persona.' He'd almost said the hotter version but decided on discretion.

'I guess so. Anyway I really am tired now so let's call it a night.'

'Goodnight kiss?' he said hopefully, but she shook her head.

'Another bad idea. Too tempting.

You're too tempting,' Claire said sadly and Rafe let her walk away.

The question was which version of Claire would appear in the morning. He rather suspected it'd be the buttoned up, full of remorse and suffering a slight hangover one. *Pity*. The new one appealed to him far too much for his own good.

7

'Before Casanova arrives with our toast tell me quickly what's going on with you two?'

Claire took another sip of tea and didn't answer her sister straight away. By rights she should be feeling a lot worse. The slight headache she was suffering implied Rafe's magic cocktail of aspirin, coffee and tons of water must've done the trick.

'Have you told him about Philip?' Heather persisted.

'Yes, when we uh . . . flirted a little on Tuesday.'

'Tuesday? You didn't waste any time.'

Claire's face heated with embarrassment. She wasn't the type to be swayed by handsome, charming men — always determined not to follow in their mother's disastrous footsteps.

Heather squeezed her hand. 'I'm not

76

trying to be mean, just to understand. Don't get me wrong I can see the attraction, he's gorgeous and got the air of mystery about him we women love. Plus, I've never been a fan of Philip. He's a decent man but he'll bore you to death before you turn forty.'

'You need to know Rafe turned me down at first, saying he wouldn't betray another man. He's honourable, Heather.' She omitted to mention last night's devastating kiss.

Her sister choked on her tea. 'Yes, right, very honourable. We all know the direction his hand was headed if I hadn't intervened . . . '

'Whole wheat toast for two. Anything else I can get you ladies?'

Claire startled and glanced up to meet Rafe's cold eyes, their usual deep warm blue close to black today. She wanted to tell him that she was trying to explain, but guessed she wouldn't be believed.

'We'll leave at ten for your tour of the Country Music Hall of Fame. You can find lunch on your own and maybe shop around Broadway then I'll pick you up down by Riverfront Park at whatever time you prefer. Tonight I'll take you out to a good barbecue joint for dinner and drop you off back downtown afterwards at one of the karaoke clubs.' He recited the day's plans in a polite monotone.

'Sounds great. We'll be ready.' Heather flashed one of her brightest smiles, the sort which normally melted any man in a half-mile radius but he only gave a brief nod and stalked off back to the kitchen. 'Oh dear, I think we've upset the hunk.'

Claire folded her napkin, biting her tongue to stop from calling out after him. 'I'm not surprised. He was no more at fault than I was, and I'm the one with the boyfriend.'

'I'm still confused about you and Philip. You've been an item for so long I thought it was only a matter of time before wedding bells would be ringing?'

Claire played with the edge of her

napkin. 'That's what he wants but to be honest I've been having second thoughts for a while.'

'Why didn't you tell me? I'd have backed you up,' Heather said insistently.

She hadn't sorted it in her own mind yet so for now Claire contented herself with a shrug. She'd always taken her older sister role so seriously it was hard to consider opening up to Heather now.

'I don't know, leave it for now please. I'm not hungry. I'll see you out in the lobby when it's time to leave.' She made a quick escape before her sister could start again.

★ ★ ★

By nine-thirty the kitchen was clean, he'd made a grocery list for later and Rafe was ready to assign the maids their tasks for the morning. Thankfully Mary-Ellen, the part-time receptionist, would be in soon to take over while he played chauffeur and caught up on some admin in between times. The hardest challenge would be juggling how to be polite but sort of ignore Claire simultaneously. Last night was a huge mistake on so many levels. Her meddling sister was right — he had taken advantage. He'd known she'd had a few drinks and plainly couldn't hold it but it hadn't stopped him giving in to his baser instincts. *Stop dressing it up. You wanted her and you were determined to have her. Boyfriend or no boyfriend. Admit the truth.* His counsellor's voice rang in his head. Dr. Williams was all about getting him to be honest about his failings and his successes. Difficulty in facing his true self was something he fought with every day. It'd caused untold damage in the past and Claire mustn't become any more fallout from his weakness.

Rafe wiped down the counter and left the kitchen. He gathered up the packets of information Anton left for him to distribute complete with city maps, coupons for discounts in local restaurants and stores, and travel size bottles of sunscreen and anti-bacterial soap — an addition of his that guests appeared to love.

He wandered out to check the inside of the van knowing there was plenty of gas and he'd washed the exterior yesterday. Rafe jumped in to check for trash, picking up numerous candy wrappers, used tissues and one red shoe from the back. Goodness knows how six women could make so much mess in a few short hours.

'The gang's all here Mr Cavanna.' He swung around as Heather's bright voice announced her presence. 'We've decided to take turns sitting up front to enjoy the view better so Pippa's your seat mate today.'

He wasn't about to ask what view she was referring to, pretty sure it was him. He made his best effort at a smile towards the plump dark-haired young woman beaming at him. Despite his disgruntled nature these women appeared

81

to consider him some sort of prize. He heard Anton telling him to go along with it. *Good for business, bro, won't kill you to be pleasant for once.*

Rafe held out his hand to help her up into the van and you'd think he'd given her a million dollars judging by her giggle. He headed around to get in the driver's side and a drift of familiar perfume stopped him dead in his tracks. Claire, today in a dreary dark green dress, stood by the side door waiting for one of the other women to get in first.

She gave a hesitant smile. 'I drew the middle seat. You've got an interesting day planned for us.'

Did she think one conciliatory comment made up for her lack of effort to defend him this morning? Rafe's reply stuck in his throat, and after staring at him for several long seconds she sighed and climbed into the van. He followed suit, and prepared to get through another day. Only four to survive and she'd be out of his life. If she lingered in his memories he'd have to man up and deal with it.

*　*　*

Claire hated to admit it, but she was enjoying herself. She'd expected the Country Music Hall of Fame museum to be tedious but the well-staged story of the development of the music genre from all the way back to the nineteenth century easily drew her in. She noticed her sister smirk when Claire lingered to stare through the glass-fronted rooms in order to watch the people working the historical archives on old recordings and documents.

'Okay, time for the gift shop,' Heather announced, poking her in the arm. 'Then lunch, and shopping.'

Claire didn't comment. She couldn't imagine buying anything here she'd want to carry four thousand miles back home again.

'I refuse to allow you to go around dressed like a barrister in court while we're on holiday.'

'But, I am . . . '

'So what. I'm a primary school teacher but do you see me wearing my usual sensible trousers and cardigans?' Heather's diamante studded jeans, low-cut pink T-shirt and white cowboy boots made it obvious that this was a non-question.

Claire wondered how to phrase her concerns without sounding priggish.

'Don't worry, we won't go overboard, but if you intend to have a fling with our delectable host you need help.'

'I don't . . . ' Her voice trailed away, and she found it impossible to carry on lying. 'What about Philip?'

Heather fixed her with the same unusual green eyes she saw reflected back in the mirror every day. 'That's your decision to make, but if you're going to enjoy the rest of our trip with a clear conscience I suggest you make it quickly.' She flashed a sly smile. 'When we get back to the hotel it'll only be about ten o'clock back home

— not too late to ring.'

She tucked the thought away and gave a brief nod.

'Come on girls, gift shop.' Heather rounded up the group and herded them off to buy tacky souvenirs. Claire followed because it appeared she was giving in to all sorts of strange inclinations today.

* * *

Well, she'd done it now. Claire turned her phone off and laid it down on the bedside table, her hands shaking. The strange thing was Philip hadn't sounded so much shocked as resigned — as though it was only what he'd been expecting. When he calmly mentioned all the good times they'd shared she'd wavered slightly, but when she'd come straight out and asked him if he loved her Philip resorted to Prince Charles' classic answer of 'whatever love is.' That'd been the decider.

Claire sat on the edge of the bed,

feeling lighter and more free than she'd done in forever. The great thing was, and Heather wouldn't believe this, she'd done it for herself. Rafe was nothing more than a catalyst. When she'd looked at it rationally if he could turn her head so easily something must've been very wrong about her relationship with Philip. The idea of being soul mates with Rafe Cavanna was laughable, but Heather's idea of a fling was increasingly tempting.

Stripping off her wrinkled clothes she headed for the shower. She'd slip into one of the new outfits she'd bought this afternoon and go and track down Rafe, using the gift she'd bought him as an apology. Then she'd make him kiss her again.

*   *   *

He wished he could take his shirt off to soak up the late afternoon sun but with all the predatory women wandering around the hotel Rafe didn't dare.

86

Stretching out on the bench he tipped his head back and let the warmth sink into his bones. There was still half an hour before he needed to abandon the shorts and return to respectable tour guide mode. Rafe popped open his can of soda and drained it down in one long swallow.

'Working hard, are we?' Claire's teasing clipped tones stood every one of Rafe's nerves on end. Slowly he turned his head and as he dragged his gaze down over her the blood drained from his brain and pooled in the one place he wished hadn't suddenly leapt into life.

What in hell's name had happened? The earlier dreary outfit had morphed into skin-tight dark jeans, a yellow T-shirt emphasising her generous breasts, and sparkly sandals.

'I hope that's not beer?' By her joking tone he knew she trusted him more than that. Rafe managed to shake his head, pretty sure he wouldn't be able to string two words together if he was stupid enough to open his mouth. He studied her again, trying to work out what else was different. He loved she'd let her hair down again, but now her lips were stained a shiny dark pink and her eyes stood out more, highlighted with enough make-up to enhance her beauty not bury it.

'I had a great time today. It was surprisingly interesting. I brought you a gift to thank you.'

Rafe couldn't think of any better gift than her approaching him again after last night's disaster. He remembered his manners and jumped up off the bench. Claire stepped closer and thrust a long pink plastic object in his hand, and he looked at it then back up at her, meeting her dancing eyes head on and sending his heart into a spin.

'What is it?'

'Good grief, with all the bugs around here I can't believe you don't know. It's an official Country Music Hall of Fame fly swatter.'

Rafe's laughter rumbled up and burst out. 'Well, bless your heart, y'all knew exactly what I needed.' He laid on the Southern accent with a trowel, loving her girlish giggle. He gestured towards the seat. 'You gonna join me, honey?' *Explain what's going on before my effort to keep my hands off you completely tanks.*

Her enigmatic smile said he was a goner.

8

This close to him she couldn't think. A musky heat rose from his dark tanned skin and the disturbing lock of hair flopped forward making her itch to push it away so she could relish the full power of his tempting sapphire eyes. Claire cleared her throat. 'I'm sorry, for my confusing behaviour and for letting Heather assume the worst.'

'I must say, sweetheart, no woman's ever given me a fly swatter as a peace offering before.' A mischievous smile crept across his face, making her think this might not be a dreadful mistake after all.

'It was a toss-up between that and the guitar cookie cutter, or maybe my favourite — the raccoon-in-a-garbage-can puppet.' Claire grinned, and he seized hold of her hands, wrapping his strong fingers around them and yanking

them up against his chest. The thin
layers of clothes between them almost
ceased to exist and her awareness filled
with his thumping heartbeat.

'You're crazy. You do know it, don't
you, honey?'

She gave a slow nod. 'I've always been
careful and thought things through before
making decisions but it appears I'm on
the verge of abandoning that philoso-
phy.'

Rafe's eyes darkened but he didn't
speak and she knew he was waiting.
Once she told him all bets would be off.
There was still time to back out.

'I rang Philip a few minutes ago and
told him I'd been giving our relationship a lot of thought,' she ran on before
he could interrupt. 'I asked if he loved
me, and he couldn't give a definite
answer. After five years I think a person
should know, don't you?'

'I sure do, but I'm no expert.'

She needed to get this over with.
'Long story short I broke up with him,
and before you say anything it's not

because of you . . . well, not really. Heather helped me to see that if I could be so easily attracted to you Philip and I clearly weren't right together.' Claire gasped as he pushed away, shoving his hands in his pockets, and glaring as if she'd just admitted to eating small children on her days off.

'Glad I served a useful purpose.' His words dripped with sarcasm and it dawned on her how dreadful her explanation must've sounded. 'If you'll excuse me, I've got work to do. Be ready at six and I'll take y'all to *Barbeque Heaven*.' Rafe strode back into the hotel before she could say another word.

Her knees weakened and Claire sunk back down on the bench and lowered her head into her hands. No wonder he stalked off. If it had been the other way around she would've felt the same if any man told her she'd been a handy tool to work out whether or not he loved his girlfriend. So far her attempt to reinvent herself was an abject failure.

She glanced at her new clothes and seriously considered changing but out of the blue a surge of righteous indignation tugged at her. Rafe hadn't even given her a chance to explain. Typical bull-headed man. She dealt with so many of those every day in her job she should have a master's degree in massaging male egos.

Claire dragged herself up to standing and sighed. Now she had to stick on a cheerful face and make sure not to spoil one of her sister's last nights as a single woman. Sometimes she hated being grown-up, a full-blown tantrum sounded good right now.

* * *

Rafe got everything organised, Mary-Ellen was installed to take care of the remaining guests and any phone calls, and the breakfast tables laid, all while his heart splintered. He couldn't believe he'd been stupid enough to fall for a pair of bewitching sea-green eyes.

Losing everything once in his lifetime plainly hadn't been enough so he'd been idiotic enough to consider risking his heart again. Maybe he should thank her for saving him from himself but Rafe didn't think that'd happen this side of midnight. With everything done he caught up on work emails from the clinic and called to check up on some of his patients. His partners were keeping things going smoothly but he missed his kids.

Outside by the van he steeled himself to see her again, determined not to betray any hint of anger, upset, or caring. He'd be polite and professional, nothing more.

'Here we all are except for Claire. She's got a headache so she's wimped out and gone to bed early,' Heather declared and Rafe murmured a few polite words of regret, all the while flooded with a mixture of disappointment and relief.

'I'll hang around at the barbecue place while y'all eat then drop you back in town and return later, if that works?'

'We'll get a taxi back so you won't need to bother.'

Rafe tried to protest but discovered she was as determined as her sister and finally conceded, remembering Anton's adage that the guest was always right.

He'd never passed up a plate of barbecue food in his life but tonight the smell of food cooking turned his stomach. Rafe sipped on a soda while they wolfed down all the ribs, slaw, potato salad and corn on the cob put in front of them. Dropping them off outside a popular karaoke club he gave them strict instructions to call if they had any problems or changed their mind about a ride home. Of course they all giggled and told him not to be a fuss, they'd come here to get away from worried parents, nagging spouses and boyfriends — not be harassed by him in lieu. The trouble was Rafe knew from painful experience what happened when you didn't watch out for the people you were responsible for.

Back at the hotel he sat in the lobby, devoid of the energy to move and do anything useful.

'Excuse me for bothering you again.' Claire's soft clipped voice drifted from behind him and Rafe jerked around.

You've bothered me from the day we met, sweetheart. Luckily the thought didn't make it past his scrambled brain for a change. 'Not a problem. Anything I can get for you?' *My body. My heart. Name it and it's yours.*

'Would you mind if I made myself a cup of tea and maybe a sandwich? I know you don't do dinner, and I'm not . . .'

'Hey, I said it was no trouble and I meant it. You feeling better now?' He studied her, noticing she'd abandoned the new look for a pair of baggy white shorts and a faded red T-shirt. Complete with bare feet and no make-up she was back to the simple beauty he preferred.

'Much, thanks, the nap helped. I think I overdid it in the sun this afternoon. My skin doesn't do well in this heat.' She rubbed at her arms and he tried not to notice the way it tightened her shirt in an interesting, sexy way. 'Unlike you.'

'It's my Italian side comin' out. I can never get enough sun and hate cold weather with a passion. Might be hard to believe but my father's family, the Cavannas, were a noble family in Genoa dating all the way back to the thirteenth century. My full name's a real mouthful — Raphael Domenico Cavanna — no surprise I go by Rafe is it?' She scrutinised him with her shrewd eyes as if he'd said something momentous. He guessed he hadn't exactly done much in the way of opening up to her before. Rafe coughed. 'Uh, let's go get you some food. I'll fix us both something since I skipped dinner too.'

'I expected you to be a barbecue fan, don't all men enjoy slabs of meat cooked over fire?' she teased in a tentative way, plainly afraid he'd snap her head off again.

'Yeah, I do usually, but not tonight.' He didn't explain, couldn't, without saying things she wouldn't want to hear. Before she could ask any more pointed questions he headed off to the kitchen and by the faint drift of perfume knew she was following close behind.

Rafe popped the lights on above the countertops. 'Take a seat.' He concentrated on getting a large plate of sandwiches made and set it down in the middle of the table. 'There you go, fresh ham, ripe local tomatoes and crisp lettuce on wheat bread from the local bakery.'

'I can't possibly eat all these,' she protested.

He couldn't help laughing. 'They're for us to share, if that's all right?'

'Of course,' Claire blushed and he had to walk away or he'd have kissed her on the spot. By the time he fixed a pot of tea he'd got himself back under control.

'There you go. You can pour me a

cup, English style, and I'll give it a try.'

She glanced over at him, holding his gaze a second too long, before nodding and picking up a spoon to stir the teapot. 'Please do me one favor and listen to me properly this time about Philip.'

The note of quiet pleading in her voice got to him. 'If you like.'

'I do. Think about it. You'd have freaked out if a woman you'd known a grand total of seventy-two hours dumped her almost-fiancé because she was attracted to you. Talk about being put on the spot. I needed you to know the choice I'd made and the fact I made it for my own sake, in case it changed things.' A flush of heat coloured her cheeks and Rafe shifted his chair closer.

'In what way, honey?' He longed to touch the stray curl inches away from his fingers.

Claire's chin tilted up. 'In case you wanted to kiss me again, but were holding back.' Her pale hands resting on the table trembled and the hint of vulnerability gave him the impetus to speak up.

'Honey, I've been holding back since the moment we met. Pouncing on female guests isn't considered good business practice, and when you mentioned Philip that sealed it. I've been the one cheated on before now and would never do that to anyone else.'

She nodded. 'I respect your reasons.' Claire gazed playfully at him from under her long eyelashes. 'Do you think you might overcome your scruples if I promise not to sue the hotel for . . . dangerous kissing?' Her low laugh rumbled right through him, and Rafe gave in.

9

The rigid restraint he'd forced himself to live by for three years failed him, pushed aside by this beguiling woman and her artless request for him to kiss her. Rafe was very afraid he couldn't refuse her anything.

He rubbed his thumb along the line of her jaw, coming to rest on her generous mouth. 'I might be able to overcome them. Is this what you had in mind?' He swooped in, replacing his thumb with his lips, nibbling and teasing until she sighed and opened to him. Rafe explored her sweetness and her instant response sent him crazy. 'Come here,' he growled and pulled her over onto his lap to torment them both with another deep, lethal kiss while his fingers worked a trail up under her T-shirt to stroke through the silky material of her bra. 'Would it be forward of me to suggest moving this upstairs before any of your protectors turn up to accuse me of being Jack the Ripper reincarnated?'

Claire blushed and he ached to send the same rush of heat zooming all over her body.

'I'll take it you approve of the idea,' Rafe declared and tipped her gently up to standing so he could swing her into his arms.

'You can't possibly carry me upstairs,' she protested, but he gave her another kiss to shut her up.

'Hey, I managed your ton-of-bricks suitcase, didn't I?'

She playfully smacked him but he kept going, out into the lobby and up the stairs before anyone saw them. Rafe tapped open his bedroom door with his foot and dropped a laughing Claire down on the bed before kicking the door shut.

The voices in his head nagged at him — they knew nothing about each other and she was worth more than a holiday fling, but he wanted her too much to hold back any longer.

'You're thinking again. What's stopping you now?' Her voice wavered. 'Have I been a fool and flung myself at you when you're not interested?'

Rafe's rough laugh ricocheted around the room. He dropped down on the bed next to Claire and seized her hand and pressed it gently against his arousal. 'How much more interested would you like me to be? Good Lord, woman, I'm barely holding it together here. If you're not careful I'll rip your clothes off and make love to you without any attempt at class until neither one of us remembers our own name.'

A flash of satisfaction lit up her beautiful face and she reached up to wrap her arms around his neck. 'As I said, what's stopping you?'

*   *   *

Through a haze of sheer unadulterated desire Claire couldn't believe what

103

she'd said. Rafe grabbed the hem of her shirt and ripped it over her head, flicked open her bra and tossed them both out of the way. He eased her back onto the bed and got rid of the rest of her clothes in record time before doing the same with his own.

Her gaze settled on him as he fumbled with a condom and saw to protecting her, grateful one of them hadn't completely lost all sense.

'You still sure?' he rasped, and she could only nod. Rafe knelt over her and a slow, easy smile crept across his face as he lowered himself, until their skin touched — everywhere. 'Look at me, and keep looking at me, I want to see what I'm doing to you.' Claire wrapped her legs around him and met his challenge with a deep kiss. Slowly he made them one and then held himself still, the corded muscles in his neck throbbing with the effort.

'I'm not made of glass,' she whispered.

'Careful what you ask for, honey,'

Rafe growled. He eased them into a steady, hypnotic rhythm all the while whispering how beautiful she was and what she was doing to him. Rafe reached between them to stroke her, tumbling her into an explosive release which engulfed every sense. From somewhere far off Claire heard him call her name and then he collapsed on her, gasping for breath, his sweat-slick body molded to her own.

Tears of relief stung her eyes. Now she understood why Heather always had such a broad smile on her face when she'd been with her beloved Tom. There was nothing gentle about Rafe's lovemaking, she should've known it'd be this way and how they'd be together.

'Damn it, did I hurt you?' Rafe's worry made her smile and she reached up to stroke his beautiful, stern face.

'No, it was amazing, I'd thought I wasn't very good at . . . this.' Heat flared on her sensitive aroused skin and he brushed soft kisses on her cheeks.

'Not very good? If you were any

damn better I'd be dead.' His blatant appreciation made her smile. 'But if I don't move off you soon you'll be the one struggling to breathe and stay alive.'

Claire wrapped her arms tighter around his back to hold him to her. 'Not yet.'

'We need to, love,' he murmured, playing with her hair and dropping more gentle kisses down her neck.

She picked up on his meaning and blushed again, touched by his thought-fulness.

Rafe raised himself up and slowly eased out from her body, the loss making her bite her tongue to stop from protesting. 'Don't go anywhere, I'll be right back.' Getting up from the bed he disappeared into the bathroom.

Laying back on the bed Claire plumped up the pillows and gazed around the small room. The only personal touches were a few things on top of the dresser — a travel alarm clock and wood hairbrush plus a silver-framed photo. She sat up and peered over to get a better look.

Her heart raced and she told herself not to jump to conclusions. After everything he'd said earlier there must be a good explanation.

'Hey, sweetheart, come here. My arms are empty.' Rafe jumped back in and reached for her, but she wriggled away.

The sweat cooled on her skin and Claire pulled up the sheet around her neck. She met his puzzled look and wished she didn't have to risk bursting the wonderful bubble he'd wrapped around them.

'What's up? Did I do something wrong?' Propped up on one elbow he fixed her with his penetrating gaze.

'I don't know, you tell me.'

'What're you getting at?'

Either he was an excellent liar or he really didn't have a clue. Claire pointed at the photo and his expression changed from concerned to blank in one second. 'Is that your family?' In the photo a grinning Rafe wrapped his arms around the shoulders of a pretty blonde woman with a black-haired little boy on her lap. He gave a mute nod. 'You didn't consider telling me you had a wife and child before you took me to bed?' She waited for him to deny it, say it was his identical twin with his family or some other logical explanation, but he only shrugged.

Claire pushed back the sheet and swung her legs out over the bed. Holding back tears she got up and found her clothes from where they'd been scattered all around the room. Her hands shook as she struggled to get dressed and out of there before she completely cracked. Over by the door she stopped and forced herself to look back at him. Rafe's pain-darkened eyes fixed on her but he stayed mute. With a groan she turned away and left.

10

As the first slivers of light penetrated his consciousness Rafe struggled to focus on his alarm clock and groaned. Dragging from the bed he yanked on his exercise clothes, fumbled around for a pair of socks and found his running shoes. He'd turn to his new drug of choice to wipe out the dull ache throbbing through his heavy, tired body. After he gave up on the prescription pain pills and excessive alcohol he'd replaced them with regular, long runs to help push the demons away.

He crept downstairs, stopped in the kitchen for a glass of water and let himself out the front door. After a few stretches he checked his watch and headed out towards Riverfront Park where he'd make the two-mile loop around the downtown green space along by the Cumberland River.

The only people around were the early workers few of the tourists noticed including the street cleaners and delivery vans gearing up for another busy day. Rafe received nods of greeting from other runners and dog walkers out to catch the coolest part of another scorching July day. Making it to the park he kept a steady pace until he got closer to the river when he allowed himself to slow down and watch the barges plying their trade as they'd done since the area was first settled. As a boy his father would weave stories around them all and Rafe had lapped it up. He headed out of the park, turning near the Shelby Street Bridge to go back across Charlotte Avenue.

As the hotel came into view Rafe cut his pace back to a jog until he reached the front door. He walked around some to cool down before he started off back inside.

'Oh.' Claire stumbled out over the step and fell up against his chest. Rafe reached out to stop her tumbling to the floor and ended up with his arms full of soft, sweet-smelling woman. It'd be an excellent way to start the day if her last words hadn't slammed back with a vengeance.

You didn't consider telling me you had a wife and child before you took me to bed?

Her face flamed and she stumbled over a garbled explanation about not expecting anyone else to be around.

'I should've been looking out. Sorry,' he murmured and eased her away, making sure she was steady before he dropped his hands to his side. Rafe became uncomfortably aware of the sweat-soaked clothes stuck to his body. 'Sorry if I got you all messed up.'

The ghost of a smile fluttered across her face. 'I'll be the same way soon, don't worry.'

He needed to get away from this inane conversation before he said something he'd regret — maybe on the lines of wanting to give her a proper explanation for his lousy behaviour the night before. 'I'm off to fix breakfast. Excuse me.' He nodded and walked away, sensing her clear green eyes boring into the back of his neck all the way inside.

* * *

Rafe combed through his damp hair and made his way to the kitchen, short of time to get breakfast organised but desperate for a large mug of coffee before he could face making a start. Last night he'd convinced himself making love with Claire was a big mistake, but thirty seconds in her company again and Rafe knew he was a moron. She deserved better than his mute silence.

He fiddled around and got the real coffee on to brew then fixed himself a mug of instant, as dark and lethal as he could make it and gulped it down. The caffeine pooled in his empty stomach and his energy level kicked back up.

Rafe focused on the list of what he needed to prepare and got busy.

The next hour flew by and he juggled getting it all done, cursing Anton at one point for deciding running a hotel was a good idea. God, a full day at the clinic didn't leave him as stressed as making sure all the guests got the right breakfast.

The noise level rose as the group of laughing English women strolled in and filled up the large table in the centre of the room. He managed to check Claire out, registering she was back in the tight jeans, paired today with a close-fitting blue and white flowered T-shirt. She looked clean, sexy and utterly captivating. *Get a grip.*

He took their drink orders and headed in the direction of the kitchen.

'Elsie, Elsie love, are you all right?'

Rafe turned and saw Mr Moody shaking his wife's arm as she slumped towards the table. He raced over, instantly noticing her pale clammy skin beaded with sweat and the way her trembling hands grasped at the table-cloth. *Hypoglycemic low episode.* 'Is your wife diabetic?'

The man nodded, his face glazed with terror. 'Please do something . . . I can't lose her. She's my life.'

Rafe checked her pulse rate. 'When did she last eat?'

'Before bed. She's just been diagnosed and we're not very good with this. I told her we shouldn't have come away from home yet.'

'She's going to be fine.'

'Should we call a doctor?'

'I am a doctor,' Rafe said quietly, glancing around at the other anxious guests and meeting Claire's confused stare. 'Get some orange juice from the fridge,' he ordered her and she took off running into the kitchen without saying a word. When she returned he asked her to pour half a glass and then helped Mrs Moody to drink. He knelt on the floor, holding her hand to reassure the frightened woman who couldn't manage to speak clearly yet.

After waiting fifteen minutes he asked her husband for her testing meter and Mr Moody found it in her large black handbag, handing it over with shaking hands. Rafe did the test and allowed himself a brief smile. 'Much better.' The sweating had receded and a little colour was back in her face. He held her wrist and counted. 'Her pulse is steadier too. She's doing okay. Drink a little more juice while I fix you a bagel and jam to get some more carbs into you. All right?'

'Thank you, I feel so much better, you've been wonderful.' She glanced around and coloured up at the sight of the other worried guests. 'Oh, dear, I've upset everyone's breakfast, I'm so sorry, I . . . '

Rafe patted her hand. 'Please, don't worry, everyone's relieved you're fine, ma'am. Sip your juice and I'll be as quick as I can. No one else will mind waiting a few minutes. Later we'll have a chat.' He smiled remembering his mother's amusement the first time she heard him using what she called his 'doctor's voice.'

He stood back up and was almost at the kitchen when Claire's voice nearby surprised him.

'Can I do anything to help, *Doctor Cavanna*?'

Rafe guessed he should resist, but needed the help and her. He nodded and she rewarded him with a sly smile as she followed, not saying another word.

★ ★ ★

Claire followed his quick, concise instructions for simple things she could do, obviously remembering her culinary limitations, while he got Mrs Moody's breakfast ready.

'I'll take this in to her and we'll see to your group next.'

Yes, and then you'll talk to me for once, you stubborn man. He didn't realise she was an expert at getting people to talk when they didn't want to.

Twenty minutes later he leaned against the counter and grinned, the hint of boyishness he rarely allowed out returning to his face. Rafe raised his mug of coffee to her. 'Cheers, boy was I ever struggling there. Anton's usually got Poppy here working with him, it's tough for one person.'

'Especially when they have to stop and save someone's life in the middle of things.' Her wry comment hit home as a sudden flash of heat sharpened his cheekbones. 'Do you normally refer to your regular job as 'this and that'?' Sometimes pinning people down worked and they caved straight away. It was the easiest and usually worth a try.

His eyes darkened to an irresistible shade of sapphire and Claire sucked in a deep breath, praying he wouldn't touch her, but sure she'd die if he didn't.

Rafe set down his coffee mug and closed the gap between them with one easy stride. He placed his big hands on her shoulders and stared down at her,

117

the heat from his body drawing her closer and setting her heart racing. 'It's complicated.'

'It's you, so it would be, everything about you is complicated.' A small sigh escaped. 'I'm supposed to be making sure my sister's bachelorette trip goes well and she goes home on Tuesday having had fun and ready to settle down to married life.' Claire really sighed now. 'Instead I'm expending all my energy falling in 1 . . . lust with a married man — great example I'm setting.'

'Honey, about last night. I'm not — '

'What time are we leaving?' Heather stepped into the kitchen and Rafe jumped back as if he'd been bitten.

Claire could've smacked her sister from here to London.

He turned away to pick up a folder from the counter and pulled out his reading glasses. As he slipped them on another ridiculous flash of desire raced through her.

In her head Claire finished his reply,

knowing it'd could've gone several ways. *I'm not married any more. We divorced. I'm a widower.* Perhaps he was Mr Rochester to her Jane Eyre with a mad wife in the attic? Her imagination devised any number of better scenarios than the more obvious — 'We're not in love any more but we're staying together for the sake of our son.'

'We'll leave here at ten and go to the Opry Mills Mall. You get a couple of hours to shop and eat lunch, then I'll pick you up and get you to the Farmer's Market in downtown Nashville. You'll have some time to look around there before your *Music Confidential* tour at two-thirty. I'll hang around to make sure you get on the bus okay and have your drinks ready to take with you. After you're done I'll bring you back here.' He frowned and read on. 'Oh, tonight's your Grand Old Opry night. Vince Gill's the host so it should be a good one. I've got a limo service laid on for you.'

Claire met his gaze and he shrugged.

There wouldn't be any time for private conversation. She must put him, them, out of her mind and concentrate on Heather. With a bright smile she clasped her sister's arm. 'Sounds great. It should be a fun day.'

Heather's raised eyebrows indicated the new cheerful version of her sister puzzled her. 'Yes, I think so. Shall we go and get ready?'

Rafe flashed an artless smile. 'Can I borrow her for a few more minutes please? I could do with some help clearing the dining room.'

Heather gave them both a dubious stare but conceded with a brief nod. 'Of course, I'll see you upstairs.' Her plain instruction made it clear Claire better not push her luck by taking too long. She left, and as the door closed behind her Rafe's expression darkened.

'Do you want me to get a tray?'

'You won't need one.'

'Aren't they handy for clearing tables?' She determined not to make anything easy for him today.

'They would be if that's what I had in mind,' he declared, and before she could protest he stepped close again.

'And you don't?' she tripped over her words as Rafe tentatively rested his large, warm hands on her shoulders.

'Nope. Be quiet.' He pleaded. 'I need a few moments with you before this crazy day gets away from us.'

'But . . .'

'After the Opry tonight meet me in the garden.'

'Are you going to ask nicely?'

'I'll do it any way you want. On my knees if necessary,' he said with a heavy sigh.

She softened despite her best intentions. 'You'd better come up with some good answers is all I know.'

'They'll be the truth.' The implications chilled her and Claire knew she'd think of nothing else all day.

11

Claire tried. She really did. Somehow she managed to smile her way through two hours of trailing from one end to another of the largest shopping mall she'd ever seen. She tried on every tight-fitting, sexy outfit her dear sister and her friends thought would be adorable on her — even buying some to keep them happy. When Rafe drove them back into Nashville to the Farmers' Market she'd volunteered for the back of the van as being within touching distance of him would make it impossible to get through the rest of the day.

Can I face the truth? What if it isn't what I want to hear?

'Claire, isn't that bizarre bus the funniest thing you've seen? We're going to have the best time ever,' Heather declared, grinning so wide it seemed likely her face would split. 'Come on, grab the drinks from our taxi driver.' She laughed in Rafe's direction and Claire couldn't resist looking his way.

She recognised the blank expression, it was his infamous — this is dreadful but I can't say anything — mask. For a second they exchanged a sliver of humour, not enough that anyone else would notice but sufficient to lighten her spirits. They'd joke about this later if either of them were in a joking mood.

Their 'Music Confidential' tour bus was bright bubblegum pink and the two musicians leading it as loud and brash as their vehicle. Heather had wanted to do the original 'Nash Trash' tour but they didn't allow bachelorette groups any more — it didn't take too much in the way of a brain to work out why. Claire guessed you knew a group had a dubious reputation when tours which allowed, and even encouraged, patrons to bring coolers full of alcohol weren't willing to have you around. With this alternative tour they'd visit all the music hot spots in Nashville and be flooded with country music gossip interspersed with songs and risqué humour.

'There you go.' Rafe held out two small insulated coolers and his fingers wrapped over hers as she reached to take them from him. 'Have fun but be careful, sweetheart, hot weather and too much to drink isn't a good combination.' She loved knowing she'd placed the furrow of worry creasing his forehead there.

'Don't worry, I learnt my lesson at the Wildhorse.'

Rafe nodded and let her go, with an almost shy smile, not a word she usually associated with him. Reluctantly she walked over to join the group, clambered on the bus and sat next to Heather. As soon as they pulled out of the market area the first drinks came out and Claire found a beer can shoved into her hand.

'Knock that back and don't argue. You have to do what the bride-to-be says,' Heather pronounced in her best teacher's voice. 'After you've had a couple you can tell me what's going on with you and the hero doctor.'

'Shush,' Claire tried to quieten her up but the other girls were too busy drinking and staring out the windows to pay much attention to them.

'You're so buttoned up I'm surprised you don't burst at the seams. Do you ever let go, Claire? I know lawyers are careful by nature but you're a woman too remember.' Heather grasped her hand and a film of tears shaded her eyes. 'Sometimes I think it'd be nice to have a sister I could share things with, maybe admit how nervous I am — scared shitless actually.' Claire stared in bewilderment as her sister finished off the can and popped open another.

'What're you scared about?'

'Getting married of course.'

She struggled to say the right thing. Heather was only five when their mother left and with their father basically falling apart, ten-year-old

Claire was thrust into the role of responsible caregiver. They'd missed out on the whole playing together, ganging up on the parents thing other siblings enjoyed. She'd gone off to university before Heather got to the stage when they might have managed to share girly secrets, and never really came back. Interrogating people was her specialty, empathy wasn't.

'But you do love Tom, don't you?' It was the best she could come up with.

'Of course I do but so what?' Heather tossed her a scathing look. 'How am I supposed to know how to be married and the sort of person who'll only do it once and do it right?'

How the hell should I know? The pain in her sister's voice made Claire's stomach churn.

'Mum and Dad loved each other in the beginning and see what they did to each other. I've heard too many stories about how Dad stifled her, tried to turn her into something she wasn't and in the end she dumped us all and ran off to 'find herself.' About a dozen men later she's still searching. Not much of a road map for a lasting relationship is it?'

Claire touched Heather's chin, forcing her to look in her direction. 'You're not our mother. Even your heart-hardened sister can see you and Tom share something special and he'd never treat you that way.' She tried to crack a joke, but now tears stung her eyes too.

'Hey, pass us some more drinks, no fair you're keeping them to yourselves.' Cat shook Heather's shoulder and laughed, tossing around her long black hair and flashing a big grin at one of the tour guides.

The other girls weren't unkind but they usually made Claire feel old and dreary, until today. Despite the awful way things ended she'd seen herself through Rafe's eyes last night as a desirable woman comfortable in her own skin and she could laugh them off now. She happily handed over a cooler. 'Help yourselves.' She turned back and paid attention to her sister again.

'Forget what I said, I'm being daft. It's the same pre-wedding nerves every bride has, nothing more.' Heather popped open another can and drank steadily until it was finished. 'Down and Dirty in Nashville. Bring it on. After the Opry I want to go back to the Wildhorse. Will said he'd be there and wants to see me again.'

Claire frowned. 'Are you sure it's a good idea?'

'Don't be priggish. I'm not planning to sleep with him but I don't see any harm in a little flirting. I thought a romp with our sexy doctor might've loosened you up, but obviously not.'

'I never said I . . . '

Heather cut her off, shaking her head and laughing. 'Oh, come off it, he couldn't wait to get his hands on you in the kitchen this morning, and you both looked worn around the edges.'

Probably because neither of us got any sleep and now I'm wondering if I made the worst mistake of my life.

'Oh forget it, I should've known you

wouldn't share anything with me, I'm only your sister after all.' Her bitterness cut right through Claire. She couldn't reply the way Heather wanted and wished they'd never started this conversation.

For the next hour she smiled and laughed, pretended to find the guides funny and joined in the singing, taking an occasional sip of lukewarm beer to give the impression of getting as tipsy as the rest of them. Claire considered it an Oscar-worthy performance.

When the bus pulled back into the market to park she spotted Rafe in an instant as he eased away from the brick wall he'd been leaning against. She gathered up the coolers and their bags, shepherded a wobbly Heather in the direction of the door, and they followed the rest of the group off the bus.

She greedily watched Rafe walk towards them with his usual easy grace and couldn't help smiling. Behind his sunglasses she'd no doubt his dark, serious eyes were sweeping over her.

She didn't need a mirror to know the rush of heat zooming up her neck flushed her cheeks a vivid shade of traffic-light red.

'Right, ladies, let's get you back to the hotel so you can pretty yourselves up for another assault on this fair city,' his silky drawl pooled in the base of her stomach and it took all her self-control not to throw herself at him and to hell with anything else.

The other girls ran over to the hotel bus, pushing and laughing at each other in a mock fight about who'd sit where.

'I thought they were drawing lots for me these days?' Rafe's wicked laugh came from behind as his hand rested at the base of her spine, spreading his fingers so she felt the press of every single one.

'The system broke down. Whoever's the drunkest will probably win,' she teased and he groaned.

'Oh, joy, what'd I do to deserve this?'

'Be a kind brother and help out your family,' she suggested and he snorted.

'Yeah, I'll string him up next week,' he groused good-naturedly.

Claire glanced over her shoulder right into his laughter. 'Has it all been terrible?' Talk about asking for compliments, she was practically pleading for them.

'Behave yourself. As if I can answer you here,' he murmured as they reached the van. 'Later.' Rafe gave her backside a light pat and Claire jumped, hoping no one else saw. *Liar. You want them to know you've got a stake in him and they'd better keep their hands off.* She wanted to argue with the crazy voice in her head and make it remember the picture of his family but it ignored her. Stupidly it stuck its heels in and insisted there was a good explanation. More than anything she wanted to believe it was right.

★ ★ ★

Rafe paced around the garden and checked his watch every few seconds.

The Opry show usually let out about nine but after a debate about whether to come back to the hotel or go on somewhere afterwards the bride-to-be won out. Claire had caught his disappointment and given him a slight shrug as if to say 'what can I do?' He'd changed the arrangements so the limo would drop them off on Broadway and a taxi would bring them back here at midnight.

He wanted his Cinderella now. Not that he was any Prince Charming. Any pretensions he had in that area died long ago, but Claire . . . she'd made all things seem possible last night. Of course it'd crashed down because he'd left a photograph on display so now he had to admit something he'd hoped to put off until they knew each other better.

She's leaving on Tuesday. How much longer were you planning to wait?

Rafe wandered back to the bench and forced himself to sit down before he wore ruts in the grass.

He stretched his arms behind his head and laid back, worn out by thinking too much.

'Is there room for one more? We're all back safely except for Heather who stayed at the club with Will, she said he'd bring her back later.'

He opened his tired eyes and Claire, frowning and worried filled his vision. 'She'll be okay, come on.' She slid down next to him and Rafe rested his head against her soft, perfumed hair and savoured being with her again. Once he spoke the moment would change and there'd be no going back.

12

'They were my wife and son, and I killed them,' he blurted out but Claire's concerned expression didn't change.

'You need to give me more than that.'

'So you can put together a case against me? It's a long story,' he sighed, 'don't get mad at me yet, please.'

'I didn't say a word,' she protested.

'You don't have to, sweetheart, I feel it here.' He moved her hand right over his heartbeat. 'I don't ever talk about this. The people who already know understand not to discuss it, and others don't need to hear anything about my private life.'

'Where do I fit in?'

'You're a rare creature — someone I ache to talk to, but it still scares me to hell and back.' The words dragged from Rafe. It cost him to admit such a weakness. 'I'll be less in your eyes, and I don't know how to handle it.'

'Trust me, please.' Claire caught his face in her hands, and rubbed her fingers over his rough jaw line. 'Tell me about them.'

'I met Vicky in medical school on one of my hospital rotations. She was a nurse, cute as all heck and crazy for me, and we rushed headlong into marriage. We never had much time together or any money but it didn't seem to matter. The trouble started when I decided to specialise in emergency medicine because it meant another three years of punishing hours. She didn't mind so much when I was done because we could afford for her to stop working.' He fought to keep the bitterness from his voice, he'd been nothing more than her meal ticket from a mundane life.

'Emergency medicine must be a real challenge?'

'It is, rewarding and terrifying at the same time — it's the front line of medicine. I was a lousy husband,

Claire. I was a workaholic and slaved away every damn hour I could. Vicky tried to tell me how lonely and frustrated she got but I was too busy to listen — at least that's what I told her but deep down maybe I didn't care enough to try to put things right.' He ripped off another mental band-aid.

'It takes two, Rafe.'

She spoke so softly he barely caught her words. 'Yeah, I know, but it doesn't make my behaviour any more acceptable.' Rafe stroked her hair, playing with the loose curls. 'We talked about separating, at least I did, and then she got pregnant.' He shook his head, determined to cut himself no slack. 'No, we got pregnant, that takes two as well.'

'Do you think maybe . . . ' Claire hesitated.

'She tricked me? Yeah, maybe, but it brought us together for a while.' He sunk into himself, needing all his reserves of strength to say his son's name aloud. 'Sam was a beautiful child and deserved better than me for a father.' The words barely made their way out of his throat, so tight with suppressed pain it physically hurt.

'I'm sure you did your best for him.'

Rafe scoffed. 'No, I didn't. I loved him like nothing else but I still put my patients first. Vicky got fed up being basically a single parent.' Unable to sit still he jumped up and paced around the grass.

'You were saving lives not running around with other women or beating up your wife. I'm not saying you don't share the blame, but you can't take it all on yourself,' Claire argued.

Why not? I'm alive, and they're not.

She patted the seat next to her and glared. 'Come back here, now.'

A faint smile tugged at his mouth and he moved towards her, drawn by something he couldn't put a finger on. 'You're a bully.'

'Nothing more than I've heard said before.'

'I believe you, sugar.' He slumped

back down on the bench and she instantly picked up his hands, rubbing her warm fingers over his skin. The sooner he got the worst part out, the faster she'd dump him and he'd crawl back to his other life. It was nothing more than he deserved. 'Vicky started seeing one of my colleagues behind my back. I found out, we argued, she asked for a divorce but I refused. Not sure why except I guess I couldn't give up on being a proper family. I promised to change, work less and be a better husband and father, but ... she laughed at me.' Remembering twisted a knot in his gut. 'Neither of us would give in so we only spoke to each other when Sam was around, and never touched.' Rafe sucked in a deep breath and gripped onto Claire's hands. 'One night I was on duty in the ER.' He stared sightlessly off into the dark lonely place he never escaped for long. 'I thought I'd seen everything, dealt with it all, but nothing prepared me for seeing them brought in ... ' His voice broke and he slumped forward, clutching his head in his hands — every one of Vicky's screams as she went beyond help, his own howling cry when the doctor treating Sam announced they'd done all they could, it all ran in a continuous loop of pain.

Claire's arms slid up to wrap around his shoulders, pulling him to her, and he burrowed into her soft, perfumed warmth. On some out-of-body level he couldn't make sense of why she still wanted to be anywhere near him.

'What happened? A car crash?'

He nodded mutely. 'Vicky was leaving me and taking Sam with her. It was raining hard, she always drove too fast and a car in front of her on the interstate skidded but she couldn't stop in time. Her car spun around and was hit by a truck. They didn't stand a hope in hell.' He pulled away and glared at Claire, fierce hot tears pressing at the back of his eyes. 'You deserve better than me, the same way they did.'

'Isn't that up to me to decide?'

Damned if her crisp, no-nonsense sheer Englishness didn't get to him every time. God, she was a perverse woman, and he fought like mad against the idea he was falling in love with her. *Falling? You tumbled head first the day she turned up in your garden, breathing fire and calling you a lazy drunk.*

'It's obviously changed you for the better. Tell me more about what you do now,' her eyes twinkled, 'when you're not hosting 'Down and Dirty in Nashville' tours?'

Rafe groaned. 'I tell you one thing, sweetheart, I'm goin' to tell Anton and Poppy to change the damn name or I'll be a no-show another time.'

'I don't blame you.' She kissed his cheek but he pulled away.

'If you still want me to . . . touch you I will, after we're done talkin', sweetheart.' Claire nodded and complete understanding flowed from her clear green eyes.

'I didn't function at all for the first six months. The good, or bad, thing about being a doctor is the access you have to every painkiller known to man. I took anything to stop me feeling, there wasn't a single twenty-four hour period where I was conscious for more than a few hours, and even those were a blur. Of course I also tossed down a poisonous amount of whisky to aggravate things. It explains this too.' He fingered the thick grey streaks punctuating his once jet-black hair.

'My God, how did you come back?'

He saw admiration where there should've been revulsion and something inside him softened. 'Anton bullied me,' Rafe admitted.

'Good for him.' Claire's declaration almost dragged a laugh from him.

'He told me I'd never forget Vicky or Sam and shouldn't expect to, but that I was alive whether I wanted to be or not and better make the best of it. He said I'd be wasting my medical training if I didn't get out there and use it. He didn't care if I went to Africa or stayed in Nashville, but I'd better get my ass in gear or he'd do it for me. He ransacked my house, got rid of all the drugs and dragged me to rehab.'

Her hand caressed his cheek and Rafe leaned into her touch. 'You're lucky to have such a good brother.'

'Yeah, I am,' he gave in to a brief grin, 'which is why I'll do any dumb thing he asks now. I can never pay him back. After I got clean I knew I couldn't go back to working in the ER. One of my friends had started up a clinic for uninsured children and talked me into joining him. People think this is a wealthy area but there's still a lot of need. We run it as a non-profit and the staff only take minimum salaries.'

Claire beamed. 'That's wonderful.'

He must rip down her illusions if they were to have anything lasting. 'It's selfish on my part. They save me as much as I do the same in return. It started as penance, but I've come to love the kids as if they were . . . ' Rafe couldn't finish the sentence if his life depended on it, which it might do, but he had his limits.

'I understand, it's okay.'

'Is it?' He wasn't sure exactly what he was asking. 'You're a smart woman.' Rafe didn't want to say his next question, but couldn't hold back. 'Am I nothing more than your fling for a few days away from normal life?'

'If I say yes I'll sound shallow, but if I say no we're both going to freak out. We've known each other six short days, Rafe, how do you expect me to reply?'

'You're right, honey, I'm a dumbass sometimes.'

'I'm not going to argue with you there,' she conceded with a bright smile. 'Don't you think we've done enough heavy talking for one night? You want to find something to take my mind off worrying about Heather?'

He sensed a thread of real worry under the light words and played along. 'What've you got in mind, gorgeous?' Rafe edged closer and leaned over to rest his hand in the hollow of her throat, trailing his fingers down to toy with the collar of her pale blue dress.

She pressed into his touch and looked up from under her long lashes, he'd swear she fluttered them at him although she'd deny it hotly. 'Well, if you can't guess you're a sorrier creature than I thought.' Her sly, teasing words slid over his skin, tightening it to the point of pain. 'By the way, I find a touch of grey hair on a man very attractive.' She played with the lock of hair which always fell out of any style he had it cut into.

Very slowly and deliberately he started to work the small pearl buttons open. His fingers brushed her soft, warm skin and a shiver trembled through her straight into his blood. Knowing he aroused her so easily turned him on beyond anything. 'We'd better take this inside.' Claire's pout made him smile. 'Don't get me wrong, I'd happily make love to you right here, but I figure you might get a touch embarrassed if we're disturbed.'

Her eyes darkened and her lips turned up in the wickedest smile. 'Heather keeps saying I need to loosen up. This trip was supposed to be a case of 'What happens in Nashville stays in Nashville' thing for all of us. Of course I didn't expect you.'

'You're not the only one, sweetheart,' he rasped, a low growl rumbling through his throat.

'I've been thinking of you, of us together, all day,' Rafe said as he pulled them both up to standing, needing her to understand how much she was getting to him.

'I have too.' He loved the slight tremor in her voice, matched by her flashing eyes, gleaming a cat-like green in the moonlight.

She arched into his touch as he stroked his fingers lingeringly down over her breasts. 'You want me, don't you?' Rafe asked on a sighing breath.

'Don't make me wait any longer,' she whispered.

At that moment Rafe knew he'd do

anything to keep this extraordinary woman in his life. Anything she asked of him.

13

As the early morning sun trickled in through the half-open blinds Claire woke up with Rafe's arms wrapped around her and sighed with contentment. He'd whisked her up to his room last night after persuading her that making love in the hotel garden might be taking her new found daring a little too far.

She itched to push the hair away from Rafe's closed eyes but resisted the urge, not wanting to wake him. These moments watching him sleep were too precious — the chance to wonder who the man was who'd touched her heart and everywhere else so masterfully. The outer shell was extremely worth looking at, but it was what lay beneath the handsome exterior that really got to her. He'd released something in her she hadn't known existed and she couldn't imagine putting the magic back in the bottle on Tuesday, leaving him with nothing but a wave and words of thanks.

'You're thinking too much again, sugar.'

Rafe's low sultry drawl crept into her awareness and a rush of heat flushed her face as he reached over and cupped her breasts in his hands, languidly stroking and setting her on fire. 'Have we got time?'

'What for?'

'Take a wild guess, sweetheart,' he teased as he rolled over on top of her, surrounding her with his musky scent, his body warm and scented with their loving.

'I didn't look at the clock.' Claire felt his smile against her cheek.

'I know, you were ogling me instead.' The satisfaction in Rafe's voice made her grin. He raised up slightly and groaned. 'Damn, it's six already. We'll have to be quick.'

'At what?' Her fake innocence didn't

fool him for a second judging by his wicked chuckle.

He didn't bother to answer, only swiftly sunk himself deep into her. All she could do was hold on as he hit every sweet spot dead on and soon she was tumbling with him into another explosive release, leaving them both gasping into each other's heat-slicked skin.

'That answer your question?' he murmured, looking so smug she'd have hit him if she wasn't so absolutely drained exhausted and exhilarated all at the same time.

'Maybe.' She tried to pretend indifference but he tickled her, laughing as she flailed helplessly under him. Rafe kept it up until she pleaded with him to stop, admitting he'd done a good job.

'Good? That's a pitiful recommendation.' He launched into another round of torment until she gasped out a single word.

'Wonderful.'

Rafe chuckled and rolled them both over, gazing right into her eyes. 'Much better.' He seized her mouth in a demanding kiss and she couldn't resist, ignoring any thoughts about her morning breath. With a sigh he clutched her tightly. 'I've got to get up, love, some of us have to work.'

'I know. Isn't it our free day?'

'Yeah, Anton always gives the group suggestions and lets them pick. Some want to go back to places they've already visited and others prefer to explore the local area.'

She ran her hands through his thick hair, toying with the heavy strands. 'While you get busy I'll shower then see if Heather's got any idea what she'd wants us all to do.' Claire nuzzled into his neck, hating to move away from his all-encompassing warmth.

'Good idea,' he muttered, but neither of them moved. Rafe tipped her chin to meet his searching gaze. 'You'll come back here tonight?' He gestured towards the crumpled bed.

'Do you really think you've given me any choice?'

'Complaining again?' He teased his fingers through her messed-up hair, wrapping it around his hand and tugging to bring her up against his mouth. 'Are you going to prosecute me, lawyer lady?'

'I usually win my cases.'

Rafe's hand slid down the curve of her spine, sending another shiver of desire rumbling through her blood. 'I'll bet you do, sweetheart, I'm pretty damn sure the judges fall for your persuasive arguments every time.'

God, she could happily banter with him all day when they weren't having wild sex — the combination was lethal. The idea of going back to ordinary after a week of Rafe Cavanna was beyond depressing. Claire forced on a bright smile, determined to make the most of the hours they had left. 'Yes, well, I can't help being brilliant. I'm off, you need to get down and cooking breakfast before the starving hordes arrive.'

He nibbled at her neck. 'You're brutal. Leave me alone to suffer.'

'I will, let go of me.' She half-heartedly pushed at him but he only tightened his grip, sinking them into another tortuous kiss, awakening every cell in her body, and making her plead for more.

Rafe suddenly stopped, dropped his arms to his side and flashed her a self-satisfied grin. 'That should do the trick. Neither of us should be able to do anything but think of the other all day now.'

'And that's good?' she complained, and he shrugged, setting off a play of muscles under his skin and weakening her resolve again.

'Sure is, honey, anticipation is the best aphrodisiac going.' He gave a long slow wink and headed for the bathroom, leaving her totally frustrated and happy at the same time.

Claire sighed and gathered up her clothes, pulling just her dress on to walk back to her room and bundling the rest in a tight ball under her arm. It'd be a long day.

* * *

'I need you now.'

Rafe glanced around from the eggs he was busy scrambling as Claire burst into the kitchen. 'I'm flattered, honey, but you'll have to wait until after breakfast,' he teased, but she didn't smile back.

'Don't be so vain.' A trace of humour tugged at her mouth and he couldn't help noticing her lips were swollen from his kisses 'I've banged on Heather's door, and she's not answering.'

'Is she a heavy sleeper?' he asked, turning back to stir his eggs and check on the bacon.

Claire scoffed. 'Not that heavy. I'm worried, Rafe, please come and open her door.'

He stopped what he was doing. She wasn't a woman to panic and make a fuss about nothing. 'Let me put these

153

two plates together and take them in and then we'll go up.'

'You could give me the key.'

'No can do, honey.'

She glared, making him aware how fierce she'd be in court when her opinion was challenged. 'Can't or won't?'

'Both.' Better she was cross with him than he let her go up alone and find goodness knows what. 'We'll go together in a couple of minutes.' He shared out the food while he spoke and gestured towards the fridge. 'Help me out and pour two glasses of orange juice, I'll take these on in.' Rafe didn't wait to see if she'd do what he asked because he knew her ingrained sense of duty wouldn't let him down.

With his new Canadian honeymoon couple settled he grabbed the set of master keys from the desk. 'Come on, love.' Rafe led the way, using his longer legs to beat her up the stairs. He fitted the key in the lock, taking a surreptitious deep breath before opening back the door.

Claire pushed past him before coming to an immediate halt. 'She's not here!'

One glance told him the bed hadn't been slept in and it didn't take a genius to guess what'd happened. Claire might not like it but he'd guess her sister had taken the 'what happens in Nashville' thing to the limit.

'Don't you dare say it,' she turned on him, the fire in her eyes flaring red-hot.

'What?'

'That she stayed the night with *that* man. Heather wouldn't.' Claire's certainty was rock-solid and he chose his reply carefully.

'Maybe he had too much to drink and couldn't bring her home.' Rafe could've kicked himself as her frown deepened, he should've chosen a better explanation than her sister being at the mercy of a drunk stranger. 'I'm sure she took care of him and I bet she's on her way back now.'

'Why hasn't she rung me? She always does.' Claire gulped, and a sheen of tears lit up her eyes.

He pulled her into his arms, rubbing his hands over her back in small circles, and her taut body relaxed against his before she suddenly pulled back. Claire focused her gaze on him and Rafe knew he'd better come up with an idea or be dead in the water.

'Do you know this Will's full name or anything about him?' he asked and Claire shook her head.

'He danced with Heather at the Wildhorse the first night. Tall, shaggy blond hair, black cowboy hat, boots, jeans.'

Wonderful. Like a hundred other men in the place.

'How about I finish the breakfasts while you talk to the other girls in your group? She may've told them more about him or called any of them if she couldn't get hold of you. Remember you had your phone turned off last night.'

She blushed and he wished he could kiss away her worry.

'Okay. If I don't know anything more by the time you finish what are we going to do next, call the police?'

Rafe hedged, she wouldn't care for his answer but he'd give it anyway. She was a straightforward woman, she'd proved that by pinning him down over his life, and wouldn't appreciate him being anything less than completely honest. 'The police won't do a damn thing about a grown woman who doesn't come home after a date unless there's proof of foul play or any reason to believe she's in danger.'

The blood drained from her face and she sagged against him. 'You think he's harmed her?'

'I hope not, honey, but I don't know this man from Adam. If we don't have anything to go on when you've finished asking the others I'd suggest we get in touch with the club and see if anyone there knows him.' Rafe ran his hands up and down her trembling arms. 'We know he's a flirt, sweetheart, but it's a huge leap from there to turn him into a . . . criminal.'

'You were going to say rapist or murderer weren't you?' She didn't mince her words. Rafe couldn't lie to her, so he said nothing. Claire gave a sad nod. 'Thanks.'

'For what?'

'Not lying.'

'I couldn't, honey.'

'Good.' She pushed away and he watched her pull herself back together. 'Right, let's get busy.'

He'd never admired her more, but if he was foolish enough to say so she'd tell him not to be an idiot in the caustic British way he loved. 'Yes, ma'am.'

Claire ran off to knock on another one of the girls' doors, and he trudged back downstairs. Rafe prayed he could live up to her expectations, it hadn't been his strong suit in the past. He only hoped he'd learnt his lesson.

14

Claire made her way back downstairs rubbing at her growing headache and sending jabs of pain through her skull. After four fruitless conversations she was more worried than ever. Nobody knew Will's last name although the general consensus was that Rafe was right; Will was local and hung out at the Wildhorse most nights. Pippa did overhear him offer to take Heather for a ride in his truck which wasn't much use given their popularity around here. No one seemed to believe her insistence Heather wouldn't have willingly stayed the night with her cowboy. Perhaps they knew her sister better than she did? She refused to believe that rubbish. The fact they didn't habitually swop secrets didn't mean Claire was wrong when it came to understanding her sister's strong moral core.

'Any luck?' Rafe glanced up from the reception desk and the sight of his worried face eased something in her — he didn't think she was making too much of this. In an instant he opened his arms and she slid right into his comforting hug. Claire rested her head against his chest and for a few moments did nothing but listen to his steady heartbeat. Calm enough to speak she started to explain what she'd found, or rather, hadn't found out.

'Bit of a dead loss really,' she complained.

'You want me to call the club?'

Having experienced multiple problems making herself understood over the last few days Claire nodded, and managed a quick grin. 'At least you'll speak the same language even if it isn't what I'd term English.'

'Now, now, if you want help I suggest you don't mock my heritage,' Rafe teased.

She glanced up at the clock. 'Will anyone be there yet?'

'They open at eleven Sunday mornings so I'm guessing someone's there already.' He checked his phone and made the call.

A ripple of apprehension ran through Claire although logically it was unlikely anyone at the Wildhorse would confess to the man being a known menace. Listening to the idiotic tale Rafe was spinning about Will lending him money and needing to pay him back made her want to scream and it took all her powers of self-control not to snatch the phone away.

'Okay, sweetheart, I'm damn good.' He put down the phone and reached over to pop a kiss on her forehead. 'A certain Will Carothers frequents the club at least twice a week, lives in the Franklin area and drives a tricked-out white Dodge Ram truck. Divorced, and something of a player with the ladies, he's a would-be country singer and works as a roadie for whoever hires him.' Rafe tweaked her nose. 'You thought I was wasting time, didn't you?

You're a lawyer — you should know sometimes direct questions don't work.'

He was right, but she didn't have to care for the fact.

'Give me a few seconds and I might get you more.' He ignored her glare and tapped away at his phone. 'Hit the mother lode.' Rafe grinned and his enthusiasm made it impossible to stay cross. 'There's only one Will Carothers with a Franklin zip code so we'll take a chance it's the right one. Mary-Ellen arrives soon so you and I can beat it then and pay Mr Carothers a visit.'

Claire's independent streak wanted to protest that she was perfectly capable of going alone but her practical side ordered her not to be ridiculous. She didn't have transport, had no clue where to go, and it'd be no help to her sister if she ended up in trouble too.

'You gotta let me help you, honey.' His quiet words brought a rush of heat to colour her cheeks, no one had ever read her so easily before. 'Weird isn't it?'

'What?'

Rafe stepped close and snaked his arms in around her waist, pulling her close. 'Knowing what someone else is thinkin'? Trust me, it freaks me out too.'

She nodded and allowed herself to enjoy being held against his rock-hard chest, surrounded by his clean distinctive scent, one she'd swear she could pick out blindfolded in a room full of people. Rafe tucked a stray lock of hair behind her ear and sighed.

'Much as I'd prefer to keep you attached to me I need to do some paperwork before we go. Will you be okay for about thirty minutes?' He glanced down at her with a questioning look.

'Be ready to go at ten,' she pleaded and choked on her words. In an instant Rafe cradled her face in his big, elegant hands, rubbing his thumbs over her cheeks in a soothing caress.

'It's gonna be okay, try not to fret.'

She gazed deep into his eyes, drawing strength from his steadiness and certainty. Claire plastered on a bright smile and ran off before he reduced her to tears.

★ ★ ★

Rafe glanced over at Claire sitting ramrod straight in the passenger seat with her pale hands clenched on her lap and radiating waves of tension. They'd driven from Nashville out towards Franklin without a word being said and he was wary of breaking the silence.

'Where do you live?'

The sudden question took him by surprise. 'Me?'

'Yes, I assume you don't normally live at the hotel, so therefore you must have your own residence.' Her sharp observation put him on the spot, the same way her opponents in court must feel. 'Is it a secret?' Claire's arched expression made him realise how strange he was being.

'Nope. I've got an old house in downtown Franklin and I'm working on doing it up.' She fiddled with the heavy gold signet ring she wore on her right hand and he knew she was wondering whether or not to speak. 'Go on, what do you want to know?'

Claire fixed her curiosity straight on him. 'Did you live there with your family?'

The words hit with a punch and he glanced away to watch the road. 'Nope.' Rafe took a few steadying breaths before speaking again, his voice sounding calm compared to the jangling in his head. 'We had a big house a few miles away in Brentwood. I couldn't stay there.'

'No memories and it keeps you busy, the perfect combination,' she observed and he only nodded.

'Would you . . . like to see it?' Rafe never invited anyone to visit, he'd even put his parents off by saying it wasn't ready for company yet. 'I mean after we've returned your wayward sister to the fold.'

'You're so sure she's all right, aren't you? Either that or you're a bloody good liar and I usually spot those a mile off,' Claire pronounced with a hint of humour.

'I'm sure you'll find her sitting on Will Carothers' front porch, drinking coffee and wondering what the fuss is all about.' He mentally crossed his fingers. Being observant where her work was concerned was one thing, but when it came to her personal life Miss Claire Buchan wasn't as smart as she thought. Rafe wasn't at all certain of Heather's safety but he'd learnt to be a good actor when necessary. Sometimes it came in handy with patients and he often used it to convince his family he'd moved on with his life.

Checking his GPS he made a left turn and headed out on one of the back roads between Franklin and Leiper's Fork. 'It should be along here on the right, honey.'

'Good, and by the way I'd love to see your house.'

'It's a date,' he raised his hand to give her a high-five and she managed a brief smile. Rafe slowed down and came to a stop outside a small weather-beaten wood house with half of its roof covered by a blue tarp. He caught Claire's horrified expression as she took in the rusty cars abandoned in the long grass, an old mattress propped against the ramshackle porch, and a child's swing dangling from a large oak tree.

'This is it?'

'Yep. You wanna sit there while I check it out?' Her scathing glance could've set fire to an iceberg. She undid her seatbelt and hopped out before he could beat her to it. 'I'll take that as a no,' he murmured to himself as he followed suit.

★　★　★

No way would Heather have willingly come here with anyone, especially not a man she barely knew. Claire was startled as Rafe's arm slipped around her shoulders, giving a quick reassuring squeeze.

167

'I'm going in first.'

'But . . . '

He pressed a firm kiss on her mouth. 'Don't argue. Please. If you hear anything that bothers you or I don't come out in a couple of minutes, call 911.'

'911?'

'Yeah, it's our emergency number.'

'I know that, but why would . . . ' She couldn't bear to finish the sentence.

'I'm being cautious, nothing more, love. There's no truck here and no sign of life but I'm not lying again and telling you she's fine.'

'That was a lie?' A surge of anger rushed through her body but for some reason a burst of hysterical laughter erupted instead. 'You should be a lawyer. No one's ever taken me in that well before.'

'What can I say?' He popped a kiss on her forehead. 'We'll talk about it later.' Rafe strode off and she could only follow him with her eyes.

Claire pressed her hands into her

thighs as she watched him pick his way over a gaping hole in one of the steps leading up to the porch. Rafe knocked on the door, then immediately turned the knob and took a step forward. He disappeared into the house and her heart thumped against the wall of her chest, the noise filling her head until she wanted to scream.

15

Nothing. He checked each of the dilapidated rooms and clearly no one had been there in a long time. Wherever the mysterious Will Carothers was hiding out, it wasn't here. Claire would want to know their next plan and for the life of him he couldn't think of one.

'They're not here, are they?'

He jerked around at the sound of Claire's anxious voice. 'I thought I told you to stay outside.'

'Excuse me for worrying about you.'

'Not enough to call 911 I hope?'

'Don't be ridiculous,' Claire protested.

'What are we going to do now?'

No more lies. 'As far as I can see waiting for her to return of her own accord or contacting the police are our only options.'

'I don't care for either one. I need to

do something but I'm sure you're right and the police won't take us seriously and I don't know where else to look.' Claire's frustration burst through and Rafe desperately tried to come up with something, anything to ease away the worry lines creasing her brow.

Ideas raced through his head. 'Think hard. Is there anywhere Heather really wanted to see but wasn't going to fit into this trip?'

'There was a whole list of places we started with and then narrowed down when we made our plans, but the main one was her having to decide between Nashville, Memphis or New Orleans for the focus.'

'What was her main disappointment when you settled on Nashville?' He hated to persist, watching his question add to the sheen of concern darkening her face.

Tossing up her hands she stalked out of the house. 'I don't know, all right,' she yelled, racing off down the gravel path. Rafe ran to catch up, grabbing her elbow and swinging her around to face him as they reached the road.

'I'm not trying to be a pig.'

'Really? You're doing a bang-up job,' she snapped and yanked away from his grasp. Rafe placed a hand on each of her shoulders and held her in place up against the car until she stopped her half-hearted struggle.

He tipped her chin up forcing her to look at him while hating the hurt anger he'd placed in her eyes. 'I barely know Heather so I can't guess, you gotta help me here.' As he pleaded she softened in his hold and he exhaled a quiet sigh of relief. A shimmer of satisfaction rippled through her clear green eyes.

'Graceland. Elvis Presley's home. She's always wanted to go there but the limited time we all could get off work meant we couldn't fit it in.' Her arms slipped around his waist, and a taut smile pulled at her lips. 'Do you think there's a chance she could've talked this Will into taking her?'

If she's as persuasive as you the man

would've walked over hot coals for her. 'Sure, I don't see why not. Any musician wouldn't need much urging.'

'How long would it take to get there?'

Before she finished speaking he'd checked on his phone. 'It's a tad over two hundred miles, so about three and a half hours of driving. We'll go back to the hotel, make some arrangements and leave as soon as we can. Keep trying to call Heather and check for messages.'

Claire stared at him. 'But you can't take off and . . . '

'Yeah, I can. You don't get it, do you?' Rafe plowed on before she could interrupt. If he didn't say it now he'd lose his nerve. 'You've got me right here.' He grabbed her hand and thrust it up against his fast-beating heart. 'I don't know what the hell to do about it and you've got me a hair's breadth from saying something I swore I'd never say again to another woman as long as I lived.'

Claire leaned so close her warm breath whispered over his skin, setting his whole body on edge. 'You weren't part of my plan either you know.'

An insistent buzzing noise penetrated his awareness and Claire shoved her hand in her jeans pocket. The noise stopped before she could answer and she frowned at the screen. 'Damn, I missed Pippa. I'll have to ring her back.'

Rafe stepped to one side and while she spoke he unlocked the car and opened her door. By the time she put the phone away and turned back to him the anxiety in her eyes had deepened.

'Wonderful. Just what we don't need. Heather's fiancé Tom has arrived in Atlanta and his connecting flight lands in Nashville around one. He was concerned by Heather's odd texts and then the fact they stopped so he's flown over to check on her. Oh, Rafe, if she was here I'd shake her, but I'm angrier at myself for not listening.'

'What're you getting at, honey?' She launched into a long explanation of how her sister expressed uncertainty about getting married. Coming to a stop she gave him such a searching look it made Rafe apprehensive. What was she going to ask him now? He was petrified of letting her down.

'She doesn't believe she knows how to be a good wife because of the way our mother behaved.' Claire sucked in an audible breath, paling under the slight tan she'd acquired the last few days. 'When I was ten and Heather was only five my mother left us. I'd heard my parents argue many times late at night and Mum always had the same complaint — that my father had crushed her spirit and forced her to become a drudge.' She glanced down at her feet.

'Hey, honey, it wasn't anything you or your sister, or probably even your father, did wrong — you understand that now, don't you?'

Claire met his gaze, her wide eyes swimming with tears. 'Maybe, but I've never had the chance to ask outright. Every now and then she'll send us an updated address, always with a new man's name attached to it — at last count she was on the twelfth one.'

'I guess she had her own problems and reasons and maybe she thought you were better off without her?'

'You're doing a hopeless job of cheering me up.' A faint smile tugged at her lips.

'Does Tom know about all this?'

Claire shook her head. 'Heather never told him. When they got engaged she insisted she was turning a new page and his love would make everything all right. I told her she was foolish, that a good marriage had to be based on trust but she swore me to secrecy and I agreed. That was hypocrisy on my part because I didn't tell Philip either. Our father rarely mentioned our mother again after she left and I suppose we've followed his lead.'

'Until now.'

'Don't look so smug.'

Rafe never spoke about Vicky and Sam either so they were even. The smile drained away and she rested her hand on his cheek.

'Sorry. We're equally as bad, aren't we?'

'Yep, I think it's a given, honey.' He dropped a kiss on the top of her head. 'Come on, we'd better get back to Nashville and re-evaluate the plan.' She didn't say any more but hopped into the car with a heavy sigh. Rafe got behind the wheel and gave her hand a quick squeeze as he started the engine. 'We'll get it sorted.'

And to think he'd expected a couple of weeks running a hotel to be a rest.

* * *

Pippa raced downstairs, followed closely by the others and Claire was instantly surrounded as they all started to talk at once.

'Excuse me.' Rafe's deep voice boomed over the chaos. 'How about y'all go and sit in the lounge. I'll rustle us up some coffee and you can catch

Claire up on what y'all know.'

She could've kissed him out of sheer gratitude. As her distress about Heather grew the years of solid legal training flew out of the window leaving her struggling to remember how to even put one foot in front of the other and walk. What a hell of a legacy her mother left; a husband so wrapped up in himself his daughters basically brought themselves up, a daughter convinced she didn't know how to be a faithful loving wife, and herself . . . She couldn't even finish the thought. Poking around her own psyche was a job for another day when all this was behind her. Claire met Rafe's quizzical stare and came up with something resembling a smile.

'Come on.' Pippa tugged at her arm. 'Let our tour guide slash chauffeur take care of the mundane stuff while we talk.'

Claire tossed him an apologetic glance, wanting to say aloud how much more he meant to her but the twinkle in his deep blue eyes let her know he wasn't bothered.

'Sure thing, run along, ladies.' He shooed them out of the hall and made himself scarce.

Pippa and the others all flopped down on the comfy chairs dotted around the room, but Claire couldn't settle and wandered over to stand by the window. She folded her arms and fixed her attention on them all.

'First I need to know if anyone's either heard anything from Heather or got an idea where she might've gone. I've got a few thoughts but I want to hear yours first.' Cat sat up straighter and gave her a wary stare. Without thinking she'd slipped into courtroom mode, challenging and spelling things out in her usual concise way.

Dead silence. She intercepted a glance between Cat and Pippa and pounced. 'Doesn't matter if it's merely an idea, tell me, I'm desperate to make sure she's okay.' The two young women nodded to each other as if deciding who was going to draw the short straw and speak. Claire wanted to shake them but clasped her hands together and struggled to be patient.

'When she'd had a few drinks the other night she kept saying she didn't know if she could go through with the wedding,' Pippa shrugged, 'we put it down to pre-wedding jitters and jollied her out of it.'

No, you didn't, she merely kept it to herself until it ate away at her. Claire couldn't make herself tell them the whole sorry story about her mother. 'Did she mention wanting to see Graceland, Elvis Presley's home?'

One said yes, another no, and the third one just shrugged.

Claire sighed as Rafe strode back into the room carrying a large tray. He set it down on the table and gave her a quick wink. It helped to loosen the knot of tension in her stomach.

'Coffee, ladies,' he announced and started to pour but the hotel doorbell rang. Rafe set down the cup in his hand. 'You'll have to excuse me, Mary-Ellen is upstairs so there's no one at reception. Help yourselves.'

She couldn't face any coffee and wandered over to the door leading back into the hall. Claire's gaze swept over the familiar man removing his cowboy hat and shaking Rafe's hand.

'Where's my sister? What've you done with her?' she blurted out and Will Carothers turned and stared in shock as she flung herself at him, arms flailing.

16

'Cool it, honey.' Rafe wrapped his strong arms around her and held on tight until she stopped struggling. 'Listen for a minute, okay? Will here came with some news.'

'I sure have, ma'am. Miss Heather's doin' fine, at least she was an hour ago when I popped her on one of them big ole planes.'

Claire struggled to understand his thick, syrupy drawl. 'Plane? Where's she gone?' She threw a pleading glance at Rafe, hoping he'd help make sense of this.

'Will told me she's flown to New York and is heading on over to London overnight.'

'We're not due to leave until Tuesday!'

Rafe held onto her hands. 'Why don't we go back in with the others and hear the whole story?'

His meaning sunk in — he didn't want to make her private life the source of interest to other guests passing through the lobby. Claire managed to nod and allowed him to lead her back into the lounge. Soon she was seated next to him on the sofa and holding an unwanted cup of coffee.

'How about you tell us briefly what happened after the Wildhorse last night?' Rafe asked Will, exactly what she would've done if she hadn't been a confused mess.

She thought she got most of his story, very glad she could understand Rafe's softer accent better. Apparently Heather convinced Will to take her home with him, which wasn't the awful house they'd visited belonging to the uncle he'd been named after, but the flat he rented in downtown Nashville.

'Don't get things wrong, ma'am, we didn't do the dirty or nothin'. She told me all about her man and I don't mess around with no one else's woman.'

His staunch declaration made her smile at Rafe, remembering his own reaction when she'd mentioned Philip.

'She needed a place to clear her head a bit, that's all, ma'am.'

Claire tried to thank him but stammered through her tears, overwhelmed with guilt for not realising the depth of her sister's distress over the upcoming wedding. Rafe's arm slid around her shoulders and he managed to do a better job of conveying her appreciation.

'We thought she might've talked you into taking her to Graceland.' Rafe's comment brought a broad smile to the other man's clear open features, and in a flash Claire knew why Heather had placed her trust in him when she felt she couldn't turn to anyone else.

'She surely did try, but I've got a gig on tonight at the Bluebird — my first and, no offence ma'am,' he nodded in her direction, 'there's no way on God's green earth I'm missin' that.'

Claire had been in Nashville long

enough to know singing at the iconic venue would be a big deal to any country musician. 'Do you know if she heard from Tom, only he's on his way to Nashville?' She checked her watch. 'In fact we have to fetch him from the airport soon.'

'Yeah, she sure did, ma'am, and wasn't too pleased. She kept goin' on about needing time to decide what to do about the wedding. I'm thinkin' that's why she did a runner because that's when she started calling the airlines. Told them she'd take any seat they had to get her out of here fast.'

Unfortunately it made sense. Now she was stuck with a panicked sister on her way to London and a doubtless equally panicked man arriving to save his upcoming marriage from crumbling. Claire stood up, in a desperate hurry to start trying to solve the worsening dilemma.

'I'll be goin'.' Carothers stood too. 'None of my business but . . . ' He shuffled awkwardly from one black cowboy-booted foot to the other. 'She needs to tell her man what's botherin' her 'cause somethin' sure as heck is and we ain't mind readers.'

'Amen,' Rafe laughed, echoing the sentiment and a rush of heat lit up Claire's face.

She held out her hand and thanked him, hearing the stiffness in her voice but unable to be any different with this stranger who'd seen her sister's distress far more clearly than she had. With a bone-crunching shake he made his leave and she leaned back against Rafe, grateful for his quiet strength.

Rafe eased her around to face him. 'I suggest we all pile into the van, we'll drop the ladies off at the Opry Mills mall and pick up Tom. Don't know what he'll want to do but we know Heather's flight details so once we give him those I'm guessing he'll try to follow her. There's a good chance he can get to New York in time to catch the same flight over the pond.'

'But, I need to tell him . . . ' Rafe

stopped her with a kiss.

'They need to sort this out themselves. Remember what you tried to tell Heather? No marriage will last long without openness and trust.' A flutter of pain crossed his eyes, and Claire bit her tongue to stop from saying the wrong thing. 'And, yeah, I know that from experience.' A faint smile lit up his eyes. 'It's the weird telepathy thing again, we're doomed, honey.'

'Why do I not mind?' she murmured, rubbing against the faint shadow of stubble grazing his jaw.

'We'll discuss it tonight but right now, we need to herd everyone up and get on over to the airport. You wanna tell them the plans?' Rafe asked. 'I'll come up with something else for them to do for the rest of the day when we've sorted Tom out.'

'You're a good man, and I'll reward you later.'

'Good. Ten minutes and we need to be on the way, they don't have time for primping,' Rafe declared and ran off before she could come up with a smart reply.

Claire turned to the girls and started to explain what was going on.

'We're worried about Heather, too you know,' Cat interrupted. 'We can't just go off shopping. That would be heartless . . . '

Pippa started to cry. 'This is awful. I can't believe she was so miserable. We're lousy friends.'

'Please don't say that,' Claire pleaded. 'I'm her sister and I didn't realise how bad things were either until it was too late. There's nothing you can do right now so try to look at it from the point of view that you'll help me by staying occupied.' She couldn't cope with their worries on top of her own right now, selfish though she knew that was.

'Well, all right,' Cat said grudgingly. 'If you're sure.'

'Thank you so much.' Claire's heartfelt reply couldn't have been more real.

Rafe sat with Claire in the van and

neither of them spoke. He'd had to rein her in again at the airport when it about killed her not to explain to Tom what'd caused Heather's craziness. The poor man seemed totally baffled and by the way he spoke was head-over-heels in love and wanted nothing more than to make Heather his wife. Now Claire was mad and punishing him with her silence.

'You've got ten minutes to vent then we need to leave and pick up the shoppers,' he said easily, tempted to move in closer for a kiss but put off by her chilly aura. 'Earlier you thought I was right but it's tough to carry off isn't it? I know not taking charge goes against your nature but you did good.'

'Well,' she snapped.

'Sorry?'

'Well, not good, I know it's the modern way of speaking but it's grammatically incorrect,' she tossed back her head, making the neat ponytail swing in the air. Rafe almost caught it to give a big tug but resisted the temptation.

''Scuse me, ma'am.' He gave a mock bow. 'This good ole Southern boy don't know no better.'

'You're impossible.' Claire's eyes flashed and he knew he had her. 'You're an educated man, so why do you want to sound . . . ' Her voice trailed away and she gave his shoulder a hard shove. 'You're teasing me, aren't you?'

'Not many people dare, do they? Works both ways though, sweetheart.' It'd been a while since anyone made fun of him, his family and friends tiptoed around his sensibilities — Anton was the only one who pushed him out of his box.

'Thanks.'

Rafe almost laughed at her grudging tone of voice, but knew better than to push too far.

'You were right.'

He could practically hear her teeth grinding with the effort of not biting off his head.

'I'll try not to crow about it,' he teased and pressed a soft kiss on her cheek.

'Good idea. Now get on and drive.' She pulled away with a fake attempt at haughtiness.

'Yes, ma'am.' Rafe flipped a salute and put the car into gear before pulling out into traffic.

Rafe switched the phone to the answering service and could only cross his fingers there'd be no guest emergencies to interrupt his plans. Heather's girlfriends hadn't felt like going out without her so they'd stayed at the hotel and all spent a quiet evening watching a movie together. Taking the stairs two at a time he flung open his bedroom door and the breath dried in his throat.

With the covers tossed back out of the way and wearing a simple white nightdress, Claire sprawled over his bed — fast asleep, her rhythmic breathing the only sound in the room.

He shucked his clothes and slid quietly in behind her to snake an arm around her waist and spoon her with his body. She wriggled against him in her sleep and Rafe's breath caught in his throat. The soft, warm scent of her velvety skin snuck into his awareness and all he could think was that in less than forty-eight hours she wouldn't be in his arms any more. He couldn't begin to fathom how he'd be able to let her go, but the idea of making any grand declaration made beads of sweat prickle on his forehead. He'd screwed up so badly before and made the decision then he'd never risk it again. Until now it hadn't been a hard choice, but . . . Rafe stroked her silky, tangled curls and let himself wonder.

'You're thinking too hard again, aren't you?' Claire's husky voice drifted up to him. 'I'm scared too,' she whispered and her brave admission loosened something inside.

'What are we gonna do?' He didn't try to sugarcoat his question, they'd gone way past that.

'Right now all I want is for you to make me forget everything for a while. We've got all day tomorrow to discuss the practicalities of having some sort of long-distance relationship, and the possibility of you being my escort to Heather's wedding — assuming it still happens.'

'Sounds reasonable, counsellor.'

'Good,' she sighed. Rafe swallowed hard, overwhelmed at her trust and praying he'd live up to it. Rafe lifted her hair up to press a kiss into the curve of her neck and she trembled against him. 'I love you.' The three words slipped out and he held his breath in case he'd gone too far, too fast.

'I love you too.'

Without another word he slowly made Claire his again until she surrounded him with her heat. With every ounce of control he possessed he made them both wait, knowing it'd be worth it in the end.

'My God, Rafe, you're killing me.' Her eyes flared and closed letting him know he had her. Rafe swallowed her cry with his mouth as he sucked and nipped at her lips. Only half-aware of her dissolving around him he let go and

193

in the fleeting second before he collapsed onto her, sweating and spent, Rafe gasped out his love for her again. This time there was no hesitation.

17

Claire thrust her phone at Rafe and beamed. 'She did it!'

He glanced up from frying bacon. 'Who did what, sweetheart?' Forking the crispy slices onto a plate he expertly cracked an egg into the bubbling fat.

'Heather of course.' Rafe's patient smile warmed her, he'd listened to her endless recitation of texts starting last night at the New York airport. Those had been cross, mad at both Claire and Tom. He'd had a break while they were in-flight but as soon as the plane landed in London there'd been another long stream of messages. Eight hours of no choice but to talk to each other did the trick and Heather was now spouting the virtues of complete openness to anyone who'd listen.

'Three guesses, the wedding's back on?' Rafe slid the egg onto the plate, added a couple of slices of wheat toast, and turned to face her. She nodded and his handsome face creased into a broad smile. 'Good. Now I've got to get this food out or I'll have guests complaining. We've got to plan something special for y'all's . . . last day.' His husky voice broke and he jerked away, rushing off towards the dining room before she could reply.

Claire rested her shaky hands on the countertop and forced herself to keep breathing. *Last day.* Who could've thought when she walked into this place less than a week ago how hard it'd be to picture leaving? She startled as Rafe's large hands spread over her shoulders and leaned back against him soaking in his unique scent and storing it in her brain.

'Go and join your friends, I'll talk to y'all after breakfast, don't make this harder on us than it already is.' He pressed a kiss on the back of her neck. 'Remember I love you.' The words trickled over her sensitive skin and a shiver of desire rippled through her blood.

Without a word she nodded and walked away.

* * *

They gathered in the lobby and Claire held back as the others chattered non-stop, arguing about the best way to spend their last twenty-four hours in Nashville. With Heather sorted out and the wedding back on everyone had given themselves permission to enjoy themselves.

'I think this evening we need to follow Heather's original plan and do the Pedal Tavern tour in her honour,' Pippa declared with a mischievous grin.

Rafe checked the folder he kept with all the group details. 'I provisionally booked you on the eight o'clock one this evening. What about the rest of the day? We've got everything from art museums, Civil War homes, a tour of

197

the symphony hall, to more shopping.'

The cacophony started up again and Claire wanted to scream at them to shut up. She caught Rafe's eye and his reassuring smile wrapped her in a big hug.

'One idea I had was to head out to Franklin. It's a small town about a half hour's drive from here. Downtown has plenty of small shops and galleries that the ladies all love, and there's several neat Civil War sites and old homes I could take you to if anyone's interested.'

A heated blush crept up Claire's face. This was his way of giving her a chance to see his house. She bit her tongue to stop from showing too much enthusiasm which might make the others wonder what she was up to.

'I vote for that. It'd be good to do something different,' Cat declared and Claire could've kissed her.

'How about we leave here around eleven?' Rafe suggested. 'There's a lot of neat places you can get lunch there

— I'd recommend *Puckett's* or *Merridee's* — they're local favourites and hard to beat. I plan on staying so I can drive you around anywhere you want.' Rafe offered up his plan and they all agreed.

Claire hung back as the others ran off upstairs to get ready. 'So, Mr Tour Guide, you did an excellent job of steering that in the right direction.' He glanced around and pulled her into his arms.

'Not professional to be caught groping the guests,' he whispered.

'Isn't it only groping if it's unwelcome?' Claire slid her hands down to rest on his slim hips. 'You think we'll manage to ditch them all for a while?'

Rafe chuckled, giving her heart a pleasant flip. 'Yeah, honey, I promise. All you have to do is profess a deep interest in visiting, say, the Carter House and I'd be floored if any of them choose to join us.' He shifted closer, aligning his body with hers and she stifled a gasp as he pressed into her, making it perfectly clear every part of him was awake. 'I'll give you a leaflet to read so you can bore them with a mind-deadening amount of information on the way there.'

'No problem,' she laughed, 'boring people is my specialty.'

He grabbed hold of her, staring fiercely into her eyes. 'You never bore me, and I'm pretty sure you'll never be able to, ever.'

'I was joking, Rafe, although in my job it's often a good knack to have. It lulls people into thinking I'm not too sharp.'

He gave a wry smile. 'They'd have to be fools to think that.'

Claire playfully poked him in the ribs. 'Remember that, cowboy.'

'Clear off and do whatever women do while I clear up the kitchen, and no, if you stay and help the last thing I'll be thinking of is the dishes.' He gave her a swift, hard kiss and shooed her up the stairs.

She'd make the most of today if it killed her.

★   ★   ★

Standing behind her with his hands jammed in his pockets Rafe struggled to wipe the self-satisfied grin from his face. The minute he stopped the van outside his house Claire went very quiet then let out a long, low whistle.

'Like it?'

'You know I love it, don't you? All the gorgeous ornate woodwork reminds me of the gingerbread house in Hansel and Gretel.' She turned to him, her eyes shimmering. 'You made it sound a wreck.'

'There's still a lot more work to be done inside and to get the garden how I envision.' He moved to rest his hand in the small of her back. 'Come on in.'

'Tell me about it.' Claire headed up the wide wood steps leading to his shaded front porch, turning to look at him.

'It's one of the newer houses in the Historic Franklin district, built in 1920 and still retains most of the period features. I restored the outside first which was in terrible shape.' The wood siding took months of hard work to mend, and repaint. He'd chosen a medium shade of grey with white trim and it enhanced the cottage, showing off the quirky design. 'By the way I don't think I told you what a bang up job you did of making the Carter House sound dull.'

Claire laughed, lighting up her beautiful face so he wanted to sweep her into his arms and whisk her upstairs and to heck with the grand tour. 'It's actually the sort of place I'd love to visit.'

'Next time . . . ' The words died in his throat and she grabbed hold of his hands.

'Yes, next time.' Her firm voice made him smile again. Rafe supposed he'd been isolated so long he couldn't believe things might be different now.

Apart from his kids at the clinic and his immediate family he'd pretty much closed himself off. Claire rested her forehead against his cheek. 'Believe. I do.'

'Why are you so sure, sweetheart?' The question tumbled out before he could consider a less brutal phrasing. 'You barely know me.'

'Are you hiding the fact you're a Mafia kingpin or a convicted bank robber?' He wasn't fooled by her light-hearted comment. Rafe shook his head and she kissed him, so fleeting and soft it might've been his imagination if it wasn't for her sly smile. 'That's all right then.'

He cleared his throat. 'Let's go inside.'

Watching her wander through the small rooms, admiring the work he'd done and listening carefully to his plans for the rest of the house, Rafe was struck by how right she looked here. He almost said it aloud but didn't want to pressure her, not yet.

'Is the master bedroom upstairs?' she asked with a guileless smile.

Rafe checked his watch. 'We've only got forty-five minutes before we've got to pick up your gang to take them to *The Factory.*'

She wandered back from looking out the window onto the back patio and ran her fingers down the front of his shirt lingering at his belt buckle. 'Is there a lot to see?'

'Yeah, tons, starting with this.' He teased around the edge of her lips and she smiled up at him.

'Where does it end?'

'It doesn't honey, it doesn't,' he growled, plunging them into a mind-bending kiss and tasting every corner of her mouth before coming up for air. 'Any more dumb questions?' Claire only grinned and kissed him again before taking his hand and walking with him up the stairs.

* * *

'Was your dreary house worth going to?' Pippa asked in a disparaging way and Claire stifled a giggle. She daren't look at Rafe who'd had to button his shirt up higher to cover up the mark she'd left on his neck.

'Yes, it was fascinating, there are still bloodstains on the floor from when the house was used as a hospital during the Battle of Franklin.'

'Yuck.' Pippa cringed. 'Let's get going. We want to get to see the shops at the converted factory Rafe told us about. A couple hours there and then we'll head back to get changed for the bicycle tour thing.'

Claire caught Rafe's eye and he grimaced. While they made love in his huge beautiful bed she'd persuaded him to come with them tonight — saying she wouldn't go if he didn't. He'd tried everything to talk her out of it but a shrewd woman always had ways to best a man and Claire was enjoying discovering which ones worked on him. Before she'd thought of flirting and teasing as bad things women like her unfaithful mother did, leading to nothing more than trouble and heartache — but now she realised it didn't have to be that way.

'All right, ladies, hop in the van and we'll see if you can contribute some more to the local economy,' Rafe joked, and winked over at her.

Claire jumped into the front passenger seat, throwing the other girls a glare that said — don't you dare argue — he's mine. *Mine? Really?* It was a daunting thought, but comforting at the same time. When Heather asked how things were going with the 'hunky doctor' she'd evaded the question, but part of her couldn't wait to have a real heart-to-heart with her sister. Of course that meant leaving Rafe and, in the modern phraseology she rarely used, that sucked. She sneaked a glance at him while he concentrated on negotiating his way through the heavy rush hour traffic. The sunglasses obscured his eyes, but her mind filled in the blanks knowing they matched the deep sapphire-blue shirt he wore today, tucked into well-fitting jeans. He wasn't a man to fuss over his looks and always seemed amazed she found him handsome, Claire could reckon upon plenty of other women who'd agree with her.

'Ogling's not polite, Miss Buchan,' his deep, silky drawl trailed over her heated skin and a searing blush crept up to flood her face.

'Since when have you been polite, Mr Cavanna?' she muttered back, pretty sure the girls were chattering too much to overhear but not really caring.

'You love me this way, honey.'

She couldn't refute the statement so merely tossed her head in fake disdain and stared out of the side window.

'We're goin' to have us some fun tonight, watching you pedal this bus thing and drink beer at the same time. It'll be one for the record books I'm thinkin'.' His hand crept across to rest on her thigh, his long fingers teasing circles on her jeans, enough to arouse without satisfying her desperate desire for his touch.

'You're a monster,' she hissed and he only chuckled before squeezing her leg and letting go.

'I'll make sure not to forget my camera.' He made a clicking sound in her direction and grinned.

If they weren't in public she'd hit him where it most hurt. He'd better watch out later.

18

Rafe lounged against the wall outside the *Corner Pub* and waited. The girls had gone in a few minutes ago en masse to use the ladies' room, and no doubt make a detour to the bar.

'Water, pal?'

Chas, their driver, offered out a bottle of cold water and Rafe seized it gratefully. 'Cheers. How do you stand this every day? Doesn't it send you a touch crazy hauling drunk people around all the time?'

'Pays the bills, and most are good-tempered. They're just out for a good time.' He gestured towards the pub. 'You in charge of that lot?'

'Kind of.' Rafe explained the tours the hotel put on and how he came to be helping out.

'The cute green-eyed one's your chick, right?'

He smothered the laugh threatening to bubble out. If Claire heard Chas's sexist description she'd no doubt smack him around the head. 'Yeah, hope so anyway.'

'Snatch her up. She's a good one.'

Rafe took another long swallow. It might be nine at night but the oppressive humidity still lingered. 'How'd you know?'

'She reminds me of my mother.'

'Your mother?' he half-choked.

'Hey, I meant it in the best way.' Chas jumped back in. 'I listen a lot while I'm driving and I can tell she's smart and funny, bit of a mother hen around the other girls, she's caring — goes a long way that does. Hot and kind — lethal combination in my book, you're a lucky man.' Chas finished his water and crushed the bottle in his hand. 'I'm getting back in. Time to round 'em up.'

Rafe touched his arm. 'Thanks, pal.'

'You're welcome. For what it's worth my advice is — don't be a dick and let her get away.' He strode off with a loud laugh, and Rafe couldn't stop smiling. Strange how someone who didn't know either of them beyond a brief acquaintance nailed it in one.

'Hey, gorgeous.' Claire's arms draped around his neck and she pressed a kiss on his mouth. 'You waiting for anyone?'

'Yeah, a cute green-eyed chick,' he chuckled and nuzzled into her soft neck, pulling her into his arms.

'Who are you calling . . . '

Rafe shut her up with a steamy kiss he felt all the way to his boots. When she'd melted enough against him he risked talking again. 'Our driver summed you up perfectly. You want to know what else he said?'

Her fake glare made him grin even harder. 'I'm not sure I do, Doctor Cavanna.'

'His exact words were — Don't be a dick and let her get away.'

Claire snorted. 'Very smooth, I'm sure. I suppose it's what I should expect from someone who steers a group of bicycling beer drinkers around for a living.'

'Hey, don't malign him, he shook some damn sense into me.'

Her hands tightened around his waist and jerked him closer, moving her hips in the tortuous way that turned his jeans into a vice. 'Really, I'd like to see that for once.'

'Claire, I . . . '

'Hurry up, you two, and stop pawing each other. You're not sixteen,' Pippa chided.

'Jealousy will get you nowhere,' Claire teased right back and promptly kissed him again. No way was Rafe about to protest so he just relaxed and enjoyed it for a couple more minutes.

'Suppose we have to go,' he murmured, 'the Pedal Tavern awaits.'

She scrunched up her face and moaned. 'Oh, joy.'

'We'll talk later when we've banished this lot to their beds.' Rafe ached to reassure her but this was the wrong time and place. 'Come on, we've got two more bar stops and a lot more loud, twangy music to listen to yet.' He grabbed her hand and they ran across the road where Chas waited patiently. Rafe lifted her back up and they got settled again on the narrow hard seats.

'Heather would've loved this,' Claire said with a touch of sadness.

The sixteen-seat vehicle, powered only by pedals, was considered *the* fun thing to do in Nashville. The guide-cum-driver steered it, and Rafe was only thankful Chas wasn't allowed to drink. Everyone brought their own drinks and the tour provided cups, a cooler and ice. He'd brought several bottles of water for himself and anyone else who'd had enough of the beer and wine being happily shared around with the other riders.

Rafe squeezed her hand. 'We'll bring her back one day, I promise.' Claire met his gaze and her eyes brightened with either pleasure or tears.

'You're making a lot of those.'

He played with her hair, she'd left it loose at his request even though she said it'd be nothing more than a curly mess in the humid weather. 'You make me want to again.' Chas cranked up the music and Rafe gave up on trying to talk. He contented himself with putting his arm around her and holding on tight. She'd understand.

★ ★ ★

Creeping down the stairs Claire's heart thumped in her chest. He'd asked her to meet him in the garden where everything began. A smile tinged her lips remembering the fact she'd called him rude and drunk the first day. She tugged at the hem of the short gold and white patterned dress Cat had persuaded her to buy in a cute boutique at *The Factory*. It didn't come down very far but she'd got a slight tan on her legs so hopefully it didn't look too bad. With sparkly gold sandals and a hint of peach lip gloss she didn't resemble her normal self in the least. As each day went by her uptight lawyer shell cracked some more, so much so Claire couldn't actually imagine going back into it.

She pushed open the door leading outside and held back for a second as her eyes adjusted to the velvety darkness.

'You're safe, honey, it's still Monday and if you remember I only eat tourists on Tuesdays.' Rafe's rumbling laugh echoed in the moonlight and her feet started to walk towards him despite the fact she didn't recall ordering them to do so. 'Is this an angel coming to see me?' He held out his hand and she placed hers in it, his long fingers wrapping around and pulling her down onto his lap.

'Hardly.'

He slid his hand down her back, sending a wave of heat through her blood. 'Just checking for wings.' Trailing back up her spine he waved the air above her head, 'no halo either.'

'You're daft sometimes.'

'No one's ever called me daft before, you Brits have some curious expressions.' Rafe's eyes darkened and she sensed the shift before he spoke. 'I'm thinkin' I might have to come hear the real thing.'

She didn't have a clue how to sound casual about his suggestion. 'Any chance you might be able to get away in a couple of weeks for Heather's wedding?' Claire tried for a bright smile. 'If you don't you'll be condemning me to be the pitiful maid-of-honour with no man in sight, marrying off her younger sister.' She rubbed against his cheek and breathed in his unique scent, imprinting it on her mind.

'I'll try. I'd only be able to stay for a few days because I've been away from the clinic for ten days now and we're short-staffed.' Rafe's large hands cupped her face as he made long languorous strokes with his thumbs. 'Honey, I'm not going to ask you something I shouldn't yet although this moonlight and you are tempting me to the edge of madness.' He sighed and she almost yelled at him to forget sense, but couldn't break all her rules in one week. 'You know I love you and want more.'

All Claire could manage was a nod.

'Maybe when we're back in your environment you'll decide it wouldn't work.' His unsteady voice betrayed him and Claire refused to hold back any longer.

'Rafe Cavanna, sometimes you're a moron. You're old enough to know when something's right so if you won't spell it out, I will.' The gleam of his white-toothed smile gave her courage. 'Come to Cornwall and if you're not ready to propose before you leave we'll scrap the whole thing. I'll go back to my boring routine life and you can crawl back into your hermit's den.'

'Don't mince words, will you?' His tickled her ribs and she broke into very un-Claire-like giggles. 'Okay, I give in lawyer lady.'

'So, what do you have planned for the rest of the night?'

'Sleep?' he teased as his fingers stroked their way up her thigh, pushing the skimpy dress out of the way.

'How dreary.'

'That's me, sugar plum.' Rafe smirked against her mouth, teasing with his tongue as he did the same with his hand. 'Upstairs or here?'

'For what?'

'What d'you think?' his intoxicating drawl ran over her skin, setting her on fire for him.

'Do I have to choose?'

'I'm always up for a challenge, sweetheart, and you've been one from the day you swanned through that door breathing fire and ice because I didn't leap to your bidding.' Rafe laughed.

'How things change.'

'Yeah, they do indeed, sweetheart.'

'You've done enough talking for now.'

'Yes, ma'am.' Rafe proceeded to follow her instructions to the letter and as she sighed into his touch Claire knew what happened in Nashville certainly wasn't going to stay there and she couldn't be happier.

Epilogue

Claire kept checking her phone for messages but there was still nothing from Rafe and the ceremony was due to start in another quarter of an hour.

'He won't let you down,' Heather said with complete assurance. 'Come and straighten this train out or I'll be walking down the aisle all one-sided.'

'I know he won't but . . . ' Claire gasped as she was swept off her feet — literally. 'My dress! You're squashing it.' Rafe's unique, warm scent surrounded her and she lost her ability to think straight.

'Sorry.' He flashed her a distinctly unapologetic grin. Rafe slid her back down on her feet and chuckled as she tried to smooth down the puffy tangerine marshmallow she'd been forced to wear. 'Nice dress.'

'No, it isn't, it's hideous,' Claire

hissed under her breath.

'You told me you'd wear whatever I chose without a fuss. This is my day and I like girly frilly things,' Heather declared with a satisfied grin waving her hands down over her own frothy lace and tulle wedding dress that sparkled with enough sequins to light up London. 'When it's your turn I'll wear whatever plain, elegant creation you come up with.'

'You look beautiful,' Rafe said with an exaggerated bow. 'Tom's a lucky man.'

'We're both lucky and we know it,' Heather said quietly. 'Claire, you've got ten minutes with Mr Yummy and then it's D-Day.' She drifted off to join the other bridesmaids who were waiting in the entrance to the church.

'Mr Yummy?' Rafe asked giving her a quizzical smile and Claire wanted to eat him up. It had been the longest couple of weeks of her life. In between calming Heather down and sorting out all the last minute wedding glitches she'd missed this man standing in front of her more than she could ever have thought possible.

'I must say you clean up well.' She trailed her finger down over the front of his dark grey suit coat making him shudder.

Rafe's eyes smoldered as he checked her out and he slid his large hands down to rest around her waist. 'I can't believe you're more beautiful than I remembered.'

'In this?'

'You could wear a grocery bag, honey and I'd still want to . . . '

She placed a finger on his mouth and shook her head. 'Don't say it now. Later.'

★ ★ ★

Rafe couldn't help grinning. The shine in her pretty eyes told him all he needed to know. He barely realised what day it was after flying in first thing this morning and then getting the train all the way down to deepest, darkest Cornwall. She hadn't been exaggerating when she said it was a long way from London.

But having Claire smile at him again made the journey worth every tiring mile. Even the distracting dress couldn't dim her beauty and he'd prove it to her — later. A wisp of her delicate floral perfume drifted his way and Rafe couldn't resist indulging in one kiss, quickly losing them both.

'I've got to go,' she murmured and pulled away.

'One minute.' Rafe halted her with his hand on her arm. Timing was never his strong suit but this couldn't wait. He bent down and opened the bag he'd dropped by his feet. Pulling out a badly wrapped package he held it out to her with a grin. 'Here's a piece of Nashville that captured your heart.'

She drew out the furry black and white object and a slow smile crept over her face. 'You certainly know how to spoil a girl.'

'Hey, doesn't every man propose with a raccoon-in-a-garbage-can puppet?'

'Propose?'

Rafe quickly dropped to one knee before he could lose his nerve and took hold of her free hand. 'I love you and I want to spend the rest of my life proving it. If you agree to make me the happiest man in the world you won't have to walk down the aisle behind your sister as a sorry old maid with no man in tow.'

Her face lit up and she giggled. 'Are you doing this out of pity?' Claire teased.

'You got me there. I even bought an obscenely large diamond so you can fool them all.' Rafe wriggled the small black box out of his trouser pocket and opened it for her to see. Claire's hands flew up to her face and tears shone in her eyes. 'No crying,' he ordered. 'You'll ruin your make up and Heather will be mad at me.'

'Put it on before I start bawling,' she ordered and thrust out her finger. Rafe slid the ring on and jumped back up to standing. 'It's gorgeous.' Claire wiggled her hand around to catch the light.

'So are you.'

Her eyes rested on him, brimming with love. 'I'm so pleased what happened in Nashville didn't have to stay there.'

'Me too, honey, me too.' Rafe's fervent reply made her smile again and he knew he was one lucky man.

We do hope that you have enjoyed reading this large print book.

Did you know that all of our titles are available for purchase?

We publish a wide range of high quality large print books including:
Romances, Mysteries, Classics
General Fiction
Non Fiction and Westerns

Special interest titles available in large print are:
The Little Oxford Dictionary
Music Book, Song Book
Hymn Book, Service Book

Also available from us courtesy of Oxford University Press:
Young Readers' Dictionary
(large print edition)
Young Readers' Thesaurus
(large print edition)

For further information or a free brochure, please contact us at:
Ulverscroft Large Print Books Ltd.,
The Green, Bradgate Road, Anstey,
Leicester, LE7 7FU, England.
Tel: (00 44) **0116 236 4325**
Fax: (00 44) **0116 234 0205**

Other titles in the
Linford Romance Library:

AN UNUSUAL INHERITANCE

Jean M. Long

Eliza Ellis has a lot on her plate. Although she teaches part-time at the local school, her passion is for baking and cake decoration. When she inherits Lilac Cottage, much to everyone's surprise, she decides to move in rather than sell up. But she also inherits a sitting tenant, in the form of Greg Holt . . . When Eliza gets involved in a new baking enterprise in the village, old memories are stirred up — and Greg knows more than he is telling . . .